DISNEY

GRAVITY FALLS

TALES of the STRANGE and UNEXPLAINED

Bedtime Stories

Based on Your Favorite Episodes

DISNEP PRESS
Los Angeles • New York

THIS BOOK
IS
PROPERTY
OF

YOU'RE A STAR

_____

Based on the series created by **Alex Hirsch**
Designed by **David Roe**

"Tourist Trapped" based on the episode written by Alex Hirsch
"The Legend of the Gobblewonker" based on the episode written by Michael Rianda and Alex Hirsch
"The Inconveniencing" based on the episode written by Michael Rianda and Alex Hirsch
"The Time Traveler's Pig" based on the episode written by Aury Wallington and Alex Hirsch
"Summerween" based on the episode written by Zach Paez, Alex Hirsch, and Michael Rianda
"Dreamscaperers" based on the episode written by Tim McKeon, Matt Chapman, and Alex Hirsch
"Gideon Rises" based on the episode written by Matt Chapman, Alex Hirsch, and Michael Rianda
"Scary-oke" based on the episode written by Jeff Rowe, Matt Chapman, and Alex Hirsch
"Sock Opera" based on the episode written by Shion Takeuchi and Alex Hirsch
"A Tale of Two Stans" based on the episode written by Josh Weinstein, Matt Chapman, and Alex Hirsch
"The Last Mabelcorn" based on the episode written by Alex Hirsch

First Hardcover Edition, February 2021 10 9 8 7 6 5 4 3 2 1

ISBN 978-1-368-06411-8
FAC-034274-21015
Library of Congress Control Number: 2020943689
Printed in the United States of America
Visit www.disneybooks.com

Welcome to the Mystery Shack!

We arrive in Gravity Falls and learn that all is not what it seems—except Grunkle Stan, who is exactly what he seems. Maybe.

WEEK ONE

TOURIST TRAPPED

WEEK TWO

THE LEGEND OF THE GOBBLEWONKER

Fitting In!

Well, I know that making new friends is what it seems! Which is fun! Of course, some friends are squishier and more huggable than others. (I'm talking about a pig.)

WEEK THREE

THE INCONVENIENCING

WEEK FOUR

THE TIME TRAVELER'S PIG

WEEK FIVE

SUMMERWEEN

Yikes!

So apparently they celebrate Halloween in summer in Gravity Falls, and they call it Summerween, and it's extra creepy. But not as creepy as Gideon.

WEEK SIX

DREAMSCAPERERS

The Problem with Zombies and Puppets

You know what else is creepy? Zombies! You know what isn't creepy? Puppets! Because puppets could lead you to true love! Maybe!

WEEK TEN

A TALE OF TWO STANS

It's All Relative . . .
and Unicorns

Aaaaaand maybe they won't. Or maybe you'll find out that your grunkle Stan has a twin brother he never told you about, and he knows an awful lot about unicorns.

WEEK ELEVEN

THE LAST MABELCORN

UNICORNS!!!
I LOVE
UNICORNS!!!

TOURIST TRAPPED

Ahhhh—summer break! A time for leisure . . . recreation . . . and taking it easy.

Unless you're me.

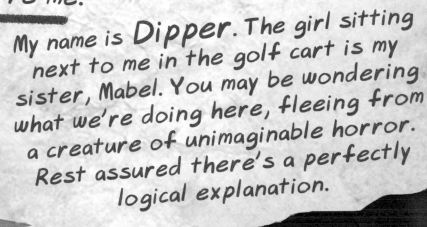

My name is **Dipper**. The girl sitting next to me in the golf cart is my sister, Mabel. You may be wondering what we're doing here, fleeing from a creature of unimaginable horror. Rest assured there's a perfectly logical explanation.

Hel-lo! This is **Mabel**. And I feel like I'm going to puke! Other than that, I don't really have anything to say right now except **welcome to Gravity Falls!**

We **probably** could have left out the part about you puking.

Probably!

For you to understand what's going on, we have to back up for a minute. **Everything** started when our parents decided that we could use some fresh air for the summer.

Whatever dreams I might have had of just hanging out and playing video games for a couple of months were tossed right out the window. They packed our bags and sent us to a little town in Oregon called **Gravity Falls.**

We were going to stay with our dad's uncle Stan! That made him our great-uncle. Our grunkle! That sure is fun to say.

Grunkle!

Grunkle!

Grunkle!

Hey, let me try that.

Grunkle! Grunkle!

Grunkle!

It's the best, isn't it?

Grunkle Stan's place was kind of old and falling apart. Our room was in the attic, and the furniture was full of splinters! I know this because I found most of them with my fingers. Isn't that great? Also, there was a goat on Dipper's bed. I think the goat really liked me.

I'M FUZZY!

But I KNOW that it REALLY liked my sweater, because it started chewing on it right away! It didn't seem like the goat would ever stop. It was the cutest thing!

My sister tends to look on the bright side of things.

Grunkle Stan had turned the rest of his house into a tourist trap—a sort of museum where people paid money to see weird stuff. He called it the Mystery Shack. The real mystery was why anyone would pay to see it.

Case in point: a stuffed "yeti" wearing a pair of underwear. Grunkle Stan called it Sascrotch.

Well, I thought it was entertaining! And he even had a mounted jackalope head! You know, the legendary creature that's part rabbit, part deer antlers on the rabbit's head. WOW!

While we were staying with Grunkle Stan, we got to work in the Mystery Shack, too!

I don't know if I'd use the phrase "got to." It was more like "we had no choice, because Grunkle Stan was making us work in the Mystery Shack."

Potato, po-TAH-to! Anyway, one day, Grunkle Stan said he needed someone to hammer up signs in the spooky part of the forest. I said, "Not it!"

So did I! And so did Soos and Wendy, who also worked at the Mystery Shack. They were both older than me and Mabel and didn't seem to pay Grunkle Stan too much attention.

Soos ↑

Wendy →

Grunkle Stan used a very scientific process to ultimately decide which of us should hang up the signs. In case you can't tell, that was sarcasm. He actually did the "eenie meenie miney mo" thing, except instead of saying "mo," he just pointed at me and said, "You."

And THAT'S how Grunkle Stan decided that I was it, so it was up to me to put up the signs. This was shaping up to be the most boring summer ever! I was walking through the forest, pounding nails, hanging up signs. But when I tried to hammer a nail into this one tree,

it sounded like metal!

I looked closely and saw it wasn't really a tree. Then I opened a small control panel and flipped a switch inside.

A trapdoor in the ground
opened behind me!

And when I looked inside, I saw an old leather-bound book. There was a handprint on the cover with **six fingers** and the number three. Inside were pages of strange drawings of creatures I had **never** seen before! The book was full of writing from a mysterious author.

Whoever wrote it, they sure were **paranoid**. They said, "I'm being watched. I must hide this book before THEY find it. Remember—in Gravity Falls, there is **no one you can trust.**"

According to the journal, Gravity Falls was full of **weird secrets** and **strange phenomena**! I could have kept on reading for hours. But then Mabel popped up. She wanted to know what I was reading. Specifically, she asked if it was "some nerd thing." Which I guess it kinda was. But I was pretty freaked out by the author's warning. So I told her we had to go somewhere private, back to the Mystery Shack. The author said to **trust no one,** but I figured I could trust my own sister. So I showed the book to Mabel.

I was all like, "Whoaaaa! SHUT UP!" and then the doorbell rang and it was time to spill the beans.

Mabel actually knocked a can of beans off the chair.

I did! Because I had some news to share with Dipper. **I had a date!** Yeah, that's right!

A date!

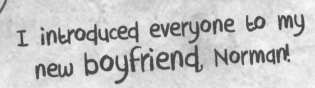

I introduced everyone to my new **boyfriend**, Norman!

We met at the cemetery, which is a totally **normal** place to meet your date. I thought he was **SO** deep!

I don't know about deep. Norman looked **pretty weird** to me. Like he said he had jam on his face, but I was pretty sure he was bleeding. He just seemed completely out of it! But Mabel really seemed to like him, so she left the Mystery Shack to go on her date.

I wanted to be happy for Mabel, I really did. But something about Norman was **bugging** me. I couldn't quite put my finger on it, though. So I decided to do a little research by looking through the journal. Sure enough, I found a drawing that looked kind of like him. The text said, "Known for their pale skin and bad attitudes, these creatures are often mistaken for teenagers! Beware Gravity Falls' nefarious ZOMBIE!"

ZOMBIES!

Was this book for real? **Zombies?** I mean, I'd seen enough movies to know everything there was to know about zombies, basically. And the most important thing I knew was that zombies weren't real! But now this book was telling me . . . they **were!**

When Mabel came back from her date, I decided to tell her the truth about her new boyfriend. After all, what kind of brother would I have been if I just let my sister get eaten by some sullen undead guy?

I opened the journal to show her, but I accidentally opened it to an entry on gnomes, which was about as far away from zombies as you could get. Then I showed her the entry on zombies. Norman HAD to be a zombie!

He never blinked!

I told Dipper that maybe Norman blinked **when HE was blinking.** Reading that journal had him thinking about all kinds of wacky conspiracies.

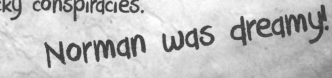

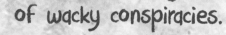

Norman was dreamy!

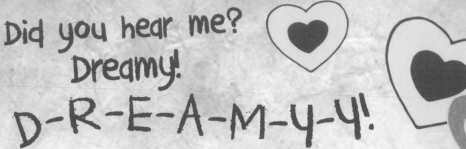

Did you hear me? Dreamy!
D-R-E-A-M-Y-Y!

See? I spelled it with an extra "y," because he's just **THAT** dreamy! I'm pretty sure you can figure out that I went on another date with Norman, who was just the perfect gentleman! When he picked me up at the Mystery Shack, he told me that I looked shiny! Oh, he **always** knew what to say.

I just **knew** that Norman was a **zombie**, but I didn't have any proof. And without any proof, Mabel was going to think that I was . . . What did Soos say? "A major-league cuckoo clock."

So I watched them leave the Mystery Shack. That was when I saw Norman's hand fall off. Norman's HAND. FALL. OFF.

Because he was a **zombie**! Not knowing what else to do, I went after Mabel.

But she had a **pretty good head start**. I was going to need some help to get where I was going. Lucky for me, Wendy was just finishing up a tour. So I asked her if I could borrow the golf cart to go save my sister from a **zombie**. Unbelievably, Wendy didn't look at me funny or anything! She just told me not to hit anybody, which seemed like **really good advice**.

Then Soos gave me a shovel so I'd have something to fight the **zombie**. And a **baseball bat**, in case I saw a piñata.

So it turned out that Norman had a secret! Oooh, I love secrets. At first, I thought maybe he was a **vampire**! I really hoped he was a vampire. That would have been so amazing! But he wasn't a vampire. He was really a bunch of gnomes wearing a human suit.

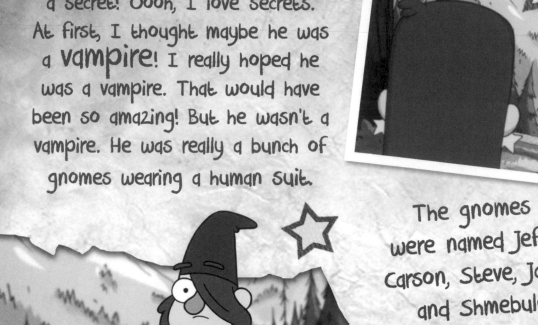

The gnomes were named Jeff, Carson, Steve, Jason, and Shmebulock, which I'm guessing is a kind of traditional gnome name.

I was still getting over the fact that Norman wasn't a vampire when the gnomes told me that they wanted me to be their **gnome queen!**

It was super flattering, but it was like, YIKES! I'm not gonna be a gnome queen. Jeff said that he understood. But what he REALLY meant was "We're going to kidnap you, Mabel!" Ugh. This day!

But I can tell you right now, **THAT** wasn't gonna happen! This is one Mabel who wasn't going anywhere without a fight. I really let the gnomes have it. And I learned something **incredibly** valuable. Who knew that gnomes would **barf rainbows** if you kicked them in the **stomach?**

I didn't! But I **DID** hear all the screaming—it was the gnomes screaming, not Mabel—and I helped Mabel get away in the golf cart. **But the gnomes chased us!**

The gnomes followed us back home, but I had a plan! And that plan, like all great plans, involved a leaf blower!

I'm not sure that **any** great plan involves a leaf blower, Mabel.

This one did! I put the leaf blower in reverse and sucked up Jeff the gnome! Then I shot him out. The rest of the gnomes ran away in terror, except for the one who was carried away by the goat that had been chewing on my sweater in the attic.

And THAT was the first really, really weird thing to happen to us that summer at Gravity Falls.

Y'know, I'd say it was The End. But it really was . . . The Beginning!

The end!

CAN YOU BELIEVE YOU JUST SPENT THE LAST FIVE MINUTES READING ABOUT GNOMES? **GNOMES!** I CAN'T STAND 'EM. LUCKY FOR ME, I WAS TOO BUSY GIVING A TOUR AT THE MYSTERY SHACK, AND I DIDN'T FIND OUT ABOUT THAT BUSINESS UNTIL LATER.

I JUST NOTICED YOU DIDN'T ASK ME WHAT EXHIBIT I WAS SHOWING. THAT'S PRETTY RUDE. INSTEAD OF READING YOU BEDTIME STORIES, SOMEONE SHOULD BE TEACHING YOU MANNERS. AND IT'S **NOT** GONNA BE ME, BECAUSE I'M NOT GETTING PAID TO DO THAT.

ANYWAY.

I WAS DISPLAYING "ROCK THAT LOOKS LIKE A FACE ROCK"! THE ROCK THAT LOOKS LIKE A FACE! BECAUSE . . . BECAUSE IT WAS A **ROCK** THAT LOOKED LIKE A **FACE!**

THAT ROCK CAUSED MORE CONFUSION THAN ANYTHING ELSE. PEOPLE WERE ALWAYS ASKING, "IS IT A ROCK? IS IT A FACE? IS IT A ROCK THAT <u>LOOKS</u> LIKE A FACE, OR A <u>FACE</u> THAT LOOKS LIKE A ROCK?"

UGH. PEOPLE—ALMOST AS BAD AS GNOMES.

ANYWAY, WHEN THE KIDS CAME BACK, THEY LOOKED LIKE THEY COULD USE A LITTLE BOOST. SO I LET 'EM TAKE ONE THING FROM THE GIFT SHOP BEFORE I CAME TO MY SENSES.

DIPPER TOOK A HAT WITH A PINE TREE ON IT, AND MABEL TOOK A GRAPPLING HOOK.

CRAZY KIDS.

THE END ALREADY.

THE LEGEND OF THE GOBBLEWONKER

Morning in Gravity Falls! Mabel and I had just finished a syrup race (you know, where you each hold a bottle of syrup above your head and whoever gets the first drop of syrup wins) when I saw something in one of Grunkle Stan's magazines.

I don't think Dipper's doing justice to our syrup race. It was epic! Also, I **won!** Which I guess explains why Dipper didn't want to go into any additional detail about it.

Anyway, the magazine was full of wild stuff! Human-sized hamster balls! Hamster balls big enough for a human! I was human-sized! Maybe I could get a human-sized hamster ball and roll around ALL. DAY. LONG!

Except what Dipper wanted me to see was an article about a **monster photo contest.**

If the magazine chose your photo, you'd win a thousand dollars and get your face on the cover! They had a picture of last year's winner, and she was holding what looked like a duck with antlers, maybe.

We saw weirder stuff than that all the time! **Like those gnomes!** But we didn't get a picture of them. All we had was our memories, and beard hair from a gnome. Honestly, I'm not sure why Mabel saved it.

Honestly, I don't know why, either! Then Grunkle Stan came into the kitchen and told us that it was **family fun day!** He said there was no work and we were going to bond.

It turned out that Grunkle Stan was really **serious** about that blindfold stuff!

He put us in the back of his car and drove us to an unknown destination. I was pretty nervous. From everything I knew, wearing blindfolds **NEVER** led to anything good.

Dipper was worrying for nothing!

The blindfolds were great. It was like I couldn't see anything! That's because we couldn't! And the way Grunkle Stan was driving, it was like HE was wearing a blindfold, too!

When we finally got to our destination, Grunkle Stan said we could remove our blindfolds. Behind us was **Lake Gravity Falls,** and we were standing next to a bait shop.

Grunkle Stan said he was going to take us fishing!

Fishing! Something we had never displayed any interest in whatsoever! I couldn't wait!

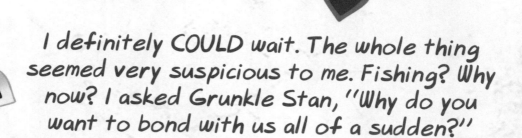

I definitely COULD wait. The whole thing seemed very suspicious to me. Fishing? Why now? I asked Grunkle Stan, "Why do you want to bond with us all of a sudden?"

I wasn't so sure about that.

The lake was crawling with people!

I mean, not literally. That probably would have been disturbing. But there were people everywhere. It was like the whole town was there!

To make the family-bonding experience even more bonding-y, Grunkle Stan gave us Pines family fishing hats! Pretty thoughtful of him, right?

Mine said "Mabel"!

Mine said "Dippy."

I couldn't believe we were going to have to spend the next ten hours on a boat with Grunkle Stan, fishing. And I REALLY couldn't believe that I was going to have to be "Dippy."

It could have been worse. You could have been "Diaper"!

That's absolutely true.

At least things got a little more **interesting** after the whole "Dippy" hat fiasco. This strange old guy came from out of nowhere, screaming, "I seen it again! The Gravity Falls Gobblewonker!" We looked at the lake to see what he was talking about. But all that was there was a fishing boat . . . a destroyed fishing boat!

The guy looked completely unhinged. It was **unsettling.**

Unhinged?

I think you mean "unhinged in a good, having-fun way"! It looked like the fella was doing a happy dance! But he was pretty quick to correct me, saying that it was a dance of grave danger, not happiness. Oh, well. As long as you're dancin', happy guy!

The man said that something called the Gobblewonker was responsible for the destruction we saw in the lake. He described the creature like this:

It had a long neck like a giraffe, and wrinkly skin like . . . this gentleman right here!

And he pointed at Grunkle Stan. He said the Gobblewonker chewed up his boat, then headed for Scuttlebutt Island.

I hate to be a stickler, but I believe his exact words were "It chawed my boat up to smitheroons and then shim-shammed over to Scuttlebutt Island."

I SAID that.

Not exactly!

YUM

Suddenly, the day was looking up! If Mabel and I could get a photo of the Gobblewonker, we could win that contest and split a thousand dollars. Plus have our faces on the cover of that magazine, which, while not exactly a dream come true, would be pretty cool. Mabel was **totally** up for it!

Then we saw Soos, who was taking out his own boat, the **SS <u>Cool Dude</u>**. Soos offered to take us along with him, which was pretty tempting.

But Grunkle Stan didn't seem too **happy** about it. He said that we could either waste time on some **epic monster-finding adventure** or spend the day learning how to tie knots and put worms on hooks with him.

We had a choice to make.

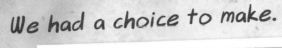

And we chose the monster hunt!

Monster hunt!

Monster hunt!

Monster hunt!

Monster hunt!

Monster hunt!

Monster hunt!

See? Even I was doing it!

So we got on Soos's boat and headed out to Scuttlebutt Island. And some people say that on a quiet night, if you listen close enough, you can still hear the chants of 'Monster hunt! Monster hunt! Monster hunt!·

No one says that. At least, I'm PRETTY SURE no one says that.

Anyway, I really wanted to win that contest. So after we made sure that we had plenty of sunscreen—because nothing's more important than wearing sunscreen—I made sure that I had plenty of cameras with me. Because do you know what the **biggest** problem of any monster hunt is?

Do you?

Camera trouble! Specifically, not having a camera. THAT'S the BIGGEST biggest problem of any monster hunt! But with seventeen cameras on me, there was no WAY I was going to miss getting a photo.

Seriously, Dipper had cameras **everywhere**. He had cameras on his ankles, cameras in his jacket, even a camera under his hat!

Soos and I had cameras, too! I wouldn't have been surprised if Dipper HIMSELF had been a camera!

How . . . how is that even possible?

I don't know!

ORANGE YOU HAPPY, MON?

I don't want to get too in depth about what happened next, but let's just say it was a good thing I brought seventeen cameras with me. Because before we knew it, Soos threw a couple of cameras away, and Mabel hurled one at a bird. Then we lost a few more.

But we still had some cameras! So the next thing we needed to do was lure the monster out so we could take its picture. Luckily, we had brought along a giant barrel full of fish food.

Soos asked if he could try some, so we let him.

Soos ate a bite, then spit it out.

I don't know what I expected that to taste like.

Yeah, I don't know what he expected that to taste like, either!

I wasn't sure how long we'd been out on that lake. Was it hours? Days? Weeks?

Minutes?

Anyway, we weren't having much luck finding the Gobblewonker in the water. The fog had rolled in, and it was getting hard to see anything. So we decided to make our way to Scuttlebutt Island instead.

And by "make our way," I mean we **crashed** into it.

"Crashed into it." Pshhhh! Dipper says that like it was a bad thing. If we hadn't "crashed into" Scuttlebutt Island, we never would have walked ON Scuttlebutt Island.

Gotta change your perspective, Brother!

YOU'RE A STAR

I WAS trying to look on the bright side, but once again, we couldn't find any sign of the Gobblewonker. What if that strange old guy back onshore was really just a strange old guy and didn't know what he was talking about!

Plus, now that I had time to think about it, I realized that we had ditched Grunkle Stan on "family fun" day. It must have been important to him; otherwise he wouldn't have gone to all the trouble of blindfolding us and driving us to a remote location. All he wanted to do was go fishing with us, and we threw him over for . . . for what? A monster that didn't even exist?

I sat down on a rock, and then something **really** weird happened. . . .

The rock I was sitting on started to sink in the water! I jumped off and watched as the ROCK SWAM AWAY. Because it wasn't a rock at all.

It was a TAIL. The tail of the Gobblewonker!

Gobblewonker alert, WOOOOO!!!

And Dipper thought we were never going to find it! It's a good thing Dipper had one of the cameras Soos and I didn't drop overboard. Right, Dipper?

It WOULD have been good, if the Gobblewonker hadn't decided it wanted to eat us! The monster jumped out of the water and knocked over a tree. It nearly crushed Mabel! We had to get back to the boat and away from the monster.

But while we were running, I managed to take a picture of the Gobblewonker. There was no way I was going all the way to Scuttlebutt Island without getting a **photograph!**

Oh! One more thing. Dipper forgot to mention that he **dropped** the camera.

The story works a lot better without that detail.

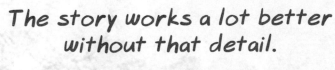

Awwww, cheer up, Dipper! At least you got to sit on a rock that turned out to be the tail of a giant prehistoric sea creature!

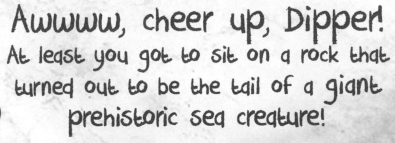

You know, when you put it like THAT, it doesn't seem so bad.

OF COURSE it doesn't, silly! Just think about all the great stuff we learned today. If we had never gone in search of the Gobblewonker, we never would have realized that Soos had his own boat called the SS <u>Cool Dude</u>! And we wouldn't have known **exactly** how many cameras you own! And that the only old dinosaur we wanted to hang out with was our **grunkle Stan!**

I'm not so sure that he appreciated the "dinosaur" comment.

It was a compliment!
And this is . . .

the end!

CAN YOU BELIEVE THOSE KIDS DITCHED ME FOR SOME WEIRD OLD DINOSAUR THINGY? AFTER I BLINDFOLDED THEM LIKE THAT? WELL, GOOD RIDDANCE! I WAS GONNA SHOW DIPPER AND MABEL THAT I DIDN'T NEED THEM TO HAVE A GOOD TIME. I WOULD JUST SPEND THE DAY WITH MY NEW FISHING BUDDIES.

ALL I HAD TO DO WAS MAKE SOME NEW FISHING BUDDIES.

THAT PROVED TO BE MORE DIFFICULT THAN IT SHOULD HAVE, MOSTLY BECAUSE NO ONE WANTED TO HEAR ME READ TERRIBLE JOKES TO THEM FOR TEN HOURS ON A FISHING BOAT. I THINK MY SOCIAL SKILLS MIGHT NEED A LITTLE POLISHING.

WHILE MY PLAN TO MAKE NEW FRIENDS MIGHT NOT HAVE GONE REMOTELY WELL, IT DIDN'T REALLY MATTER. IN THE END, I GUESS THE WHOLE MONSTER HUNT WENT BELLY-UP, BECAUSE THE KIDS EVENTUALLY CAME BACK. THEY SAID THEY WANTED TO FISH WITH ME. WHAT WAS I, SECOND PRIZE?

I DIDN'T WANT THEIR SYMPATHY!

BUT I _DID_ WANT THEIR COMPANY, BECAUSE THE FISHING BOAT WAS GETTIN' KIND OF LONELY. AND IT WAS FAMILY FUN DAY, AFTER ALL. SO I TOLD 'EM THEY COULD COME ABOARD, AND THEN WE TOOK A PICTURE, AND PROBABLY SOME OTHER STUFF HAPPENED, TOO.

THE END.

THE INCONVENIENCING

Dipper's in love! Dipper's in love!
Dipper's in L-O-V—

I am **NOT** in love! Wendy and I are just friends, okay? And I just thought it would be really, I don't know, cool to hang out with her and the older kids for an afternoon. Wendy asked how old we were, and I maybe lied a little and said we were thirteen, which was almost true.

"Almost true" is not the same thing as "true true."

Is that **really** important right now? No. What IS important is that Wendy said she liked my "moxie." That . . . that's good, right? It sounds good.

I think it's good.

Dipper's in love.

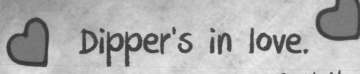

Quit it, Mabel!

When the Mystery Shack closed that afternoon, Wendy agreed that Mabel and I could hang out with her friends, which was awesome, because that meant I could spend time with Wendy! As friends! Anyway, we went outside and met Lee, Nate, Robbie, Tambry, and Thompson.

Thompson seemed pretty interesting, mainly because he was being held up by two of his friends while Robbie tried to throw candy into his belly button. I'm not gonna lie, it was weird. But compared to a bunch of gnomes pretending to be a teenager?

Not SO weird.

The other kids sort of looked at us funny. At first, I thought it was because Mabel showed everyone that she chewed her gum so it looked like a brain. But then Wendy's friend Robbie asked her . . .

That was kind of **embarrassing**. But she stuck up for us, and soon we were sitting in the back of Thompson's van, probably heading somewhere **really cool!**

I saw that someone had written some **mean stuff** in the back of the van. So I took the opportunity to write something nice!

Did I say "somewhere really cool"? Because they didn't take us somewhere really cool. They took us to a condemned convenience store called Dusk 2 Dawn. It looked like every bad thing that could ever happen to a person happened there. The word "eerie" doesn't even begin to describe the place.

I'm serious! Lee even said that the place was haunted because of bad stuff that happened there a long time ago. It had been closed ever since.

OOOOOOOOO . . . SPOOOOOOOOKY!

I couldn't believe we were going in there, and I said as much. But Wendy was all like, "Chill out, man. It's not as bad as it looks."

I'm not sure if I **actually** believed her, but I guessed the whole point of going to a place like that was to go inside. So we snuck over a fence and walked up to the front doors. They were locked, of course, and when I tried to open them, one of the teenagers made fun of me. Wendy said they should leave me alone, because I was " just a little kid."

A little kid?

Uh-uh, no way!

Bad enough Robbie already thought that Wendy was **babysitting** me. I was gonna show them. So I climbed onto the roof and saw an air duct. I punched open the grate. I was gonna crawl inside and open the door that way!

BAM!

I was inside and—BAM!—I opened the front door.

The other kids were really surprised. They didn't think I could do it, but I did! To tell you the truth, I was kind of surprised myself. Lee said, "Good call inviting this little maniac!" No one had ever called me a maniac before. And Nate even gave me my own cool nickname: Dr. Funtimes! I'd never been a doctor before. Or called "fun"!

It felt pretty great!

But then we started looking around the place, and I felt a little not-so-great.

The place looked even creepier on the inside than it did from the outside. I guess that's how creepy things work! It looked like no one had set foot in the store for at least twenty years. There were cobwebs everywhere, and everything was covered in a thick layer of dust.

And wait—it gets even spookier! You know the take a penny tray? The one where, like, if you're short by a penny, you can take a penny to pay for something? Well, there were still pennies in there!
You heard me: they were like pennies
from beyond the grave!

I'm pretty sure they were just
ordinary pennies, Mabel.
Says you.

I know we shouldn't have been inside, and I was
really kind of scared. But it just felt so good
to be hanging out with the cool kids, even if it
was only for one night. We did all kinds of stuff
you could **NEVER** do in a convenience store that
hadn't been condemned. We ran around having
food fights, even throwing water balloons
full of some kind of food
at each other!

At least, I **think** it was food. But it
was all in good fun, and I still felt like
one of the cool kids.

You wanna talk about things you shouldn't do? Okay, let's talk about things you shouldn't do! I was running around the store, having the time of my life, when I saw it: an entire display of **Smile Dip candy!** That stuff hadn't been sold for years. I heard it was even **banned!** I knew right then that I had to have some.

Not convinced?
The display featured two cute-as-can-be puppies called **Das Flavör Pups.** If you think I'm able to resist cute puppies, then I can't help you. You should just stop reading this book right now.

Everyone seemed to be having a great time. Wendy even turned to me and said that the night was legendary.

Legendary!

She told me that her friend Tambry pretty much always had her face buried in her phone. But **that night**, she was looking up! Talking to people! Even the guys were bonding, goofing off, and having a blast. And no one had said another word about Wendy babysitting me! I had never experienced **anything** quite like this before, and I loved it.

I **hoped** that Mabel was having as good a time as I was. And when I looked at her, I could tell that she was really into it, too!

I guess you could say that I was "into it." If you consider eating an entire display's worth of Smile Dip "into it"!

Now that I think about it, do you think there's such a thing as having TOO MUCH Smile Dip?

If there is, then I'm pretty sure I did it. My tummy felt like the complete opposite of "yay." It was more like, "Booooo, Mabel, boooooooo." And I don't like it when my tummy talks back to me like that.

No more Smile Dip for THIS girl!

Y'know, there's probably a really good reason that stuff was banned.

I doubt it!

Then Wendy said something really cool. She told me that at first, she wasn't sure if I could hang with her crew. She thought maybe I was a little on the young side. But after everything she saw that night? Wendy said I was "surprisingly mature" for my age. That night was amazing!

I looked around and saw that Nate and Lee were pouring bags of ice into Thompson's pants. That was slightly less amazing, but I wasn't gonna ask. They said they needed more ice, so I walked back to the freezer to get some.

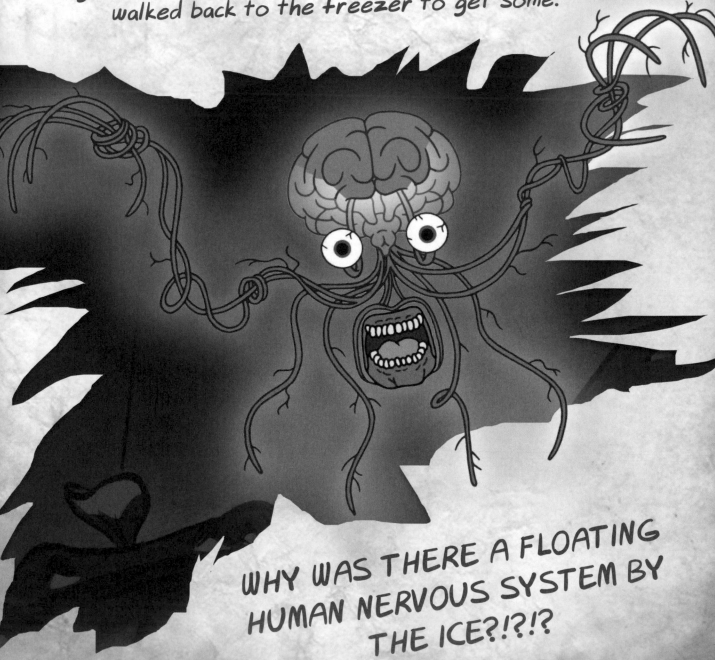

WHY WAS THERE A FLOATING HUMAN NERVOUS SYSTEM BY THE ICE?!?!?

Was it ghosts? I bet it was ghosts! I had to warn everyone! But if I told Wendy, she'd think I was acting like a little kid! As it was, I shrieked, and Lee said, "I thought I heard some lady screaming back here." So I tried to tell Mabel, but she wasn't listening.

I was so afraid of everyone thinking I was, like, Captain Buzzkill instead of Dr. Funtimes just because I thought the place might really be haunted. But as it turned out, soon **everyone** would believe me! Because it turned out the people who owned the store had died there.

And now their **ghosts** were haunting the place!

The ghosts wouldn't let us leave. We were all trapped inside the creepy condemned convenience store!

And then the ghosts REALLY started to mess with us.

They locked **Tambry** in a **security camera!**

Then they trapped **Thompson** in a **video game.**

And somehow, **Lee** became **part of a cereal box!**

Why was this happening?

Wendy's friends hadn't done anything—I mean, other than walk right into a condemned building. They were just acting like annoying teenagers.

That was when it hit me!

The ghosts didn't like teenagers! That was the only explanation! The only way we were going to get out of there was if I told the truth. Swallowing my pride, I told them that I wasn't really a teenager yet. Suddenly, the ghosts appeared, and they were super nice! To me, anyway. They said that teenagers always used to mess with their store. So when they died, they returned to haunt the place and messed with any teenagers who dared to enter.

I asked the ghosts if there was anything I could do to make them let my friends go. They thought about it for a moment, and then they said there was one thing. . . .

If you guessed that one thing was dressing in a ghostly lamb costume and doing something called "The Lamby Lamby Dance," then there is probably something wrong with you. Because that's a strangely specific guess.

Also, you would be right.

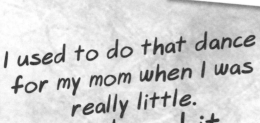

I used to do that dance for my mom when I was really little. **She loved it.** So I did it for the two ghosts, and it made them so **happy** they let everyone go.

Mabel was slowly starting to feel better, and she swore off eating banned candy for the rest of her life. We both agreed that the next time we hung out with Wendy, it **wasn't** gonna be at some **creepy condemned convenience store!**

The end!

LOOK, I MAY NOT KNOW MUCH, BUT IF THERE'S ANYTHING I'VE LEARNED FROM MY TIME ON THIS ROCK, IT'S THAT SMILE DIP IS **BAD NEWS**. YOU EAT SMILE DIP AT YOUR OWN PERIL. WANNA FEEL CRUMMY? EAT SMILE DIP. IN OTHER WORDS,

DO NOT EAT SMILE DIP.

ALSO, IF YOU **TELL PEOPLE** NAMED WENDY AND SOOS THAT THEY GOTTA CLEAN THE BATHROOM, ODDS ARE PRETTY GOOD THEY'RE NOT GONNA DO IT. NOW THAT I THINK ABOUT IT, IF YOU TELL **ANYONE** TO CLEAN THE BATHROOM, THEY PROBABLY WON'T DO IT. ANYWAY, THE **SOONER** YOU LEARN THAT, THE **BETTER**. THAT WAY YOU CAN MANAGE THE DISAPPOINTMENT!

OH, AND ONE MORE THING! SAY YOU'RE SITTING AT HOME, ENJOYING A NICE QUIET NIGHT OF PUBLIC ACCESS TV. MAYBE YOU'RE WATCHING A SHOW ALL ABOUT GULCHES! THEY GOT THINGS LIKE THAT, RIGHT?

ANYWAY, THAT SHOW'S PROBABLY PRETTY BORING. YOU WANNA TURN THE CHANNEL, BUT YOU CAN'T FIND THE REMOTE. SO YOU ASK TWO KIDS—MAYBE THEIR NAMES RHYME WITH MIPPER AND DABEL—TO FIND IT. BUT THEY'RE NOT THERE! BECAUSE THEY WENT OUT TO HAVE FUN WHILE SELFISHLY LEAVING YOU WITH NO POSSIBLE WAY OF CHANGING THE CHANNEL EXCEPT GETTING UP!

AND WHO'S GONNA DO THAT? HUH? WHO?!?

THAT'S THE END, I GUESS.

THE TIME TRAVELER'S PIG

Have you ever been to the Mystery Fair?

Of course you haven't. That's because you've never met our grunkle Stan. To make a little extra money, Grunkle Stan set up the Mystery Fair on the yard behind the Mystery Shack. It had some of the stuff you'd expect to see at a fair—y'know, like a Ferris wheel, poorly constructed game booths designed to cheat people, and some pretty smelly portable toilets.

Dipper's description doesn't begin to do the Mystery Fair justice! It was magical! Grunkle Stan called it "the cheapest fair money can rent"! He said that he spared EVERY EXPENSE!

He even gave us jobs to do.

By " jobs," Mabel means that Grunkle Stan handed us a stack of fake safety inspection certificates and told us to put them on anything that looked like an **accident** waiting to happen. Like the sky tram, which was broken, along with most of my bones when I tested it out.

I think Grunkle Stan was most proud of his "Dunkle the Grunkle" tank, which was one of those dunk tanks. Except Soos rigged it so Grunkle Stan couldn't be dunked. He was really happy about that, because it meant he could take everyone's money and **never** get wet.

I was actually **surprised** by the number of people who turned out for the Mystery Fair. **The place was really busy!**

After my experience on the tram, and especially after Grunkle Stan told us to use fewer nails when hammering everything together, I wasn't in a hurry to go on any rides. So I hung out with Wendy. I mean, I asked her to hang out with me at the fair—**which was amazing!** I just went right up to her and said, "Hey, you wanna hang out at the fair?" And you know what she said?

She said, "Yeah, I guess so."

How cool is that?!?!?

And we got corn dogs. Or "mystery dogs," as Grunkle Stan called them. They were corn dogs in the shape of a question mark. The big mystery was, how did he GET them in the shape of a question mark? **It was unnatural!**

I think you mean unnatural-ly **FUN!**

Dipper was **finally** taking some chances and getting to know Wendy. I knew things would work out if he followed my advice, because I'm **always** right!

Like when I said, "Do you smell a gallon of body spray?" I was right about that, because Wendy's friend Robbie walked over to us,

smelling like—drumroll, please—**a gallon of body spray!**

Ugh, THAT guy. First thing he said was . . .

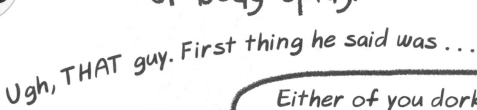

Either of you dorks seen Wendy around?

Then he took a bunch of Mabel's **cotton candy!** Jerk.
He said he wanted to show Wendy his new jeans. So I told him that I'd seen Wendy in the bottomless pit, and that maybe he should go jump in there.

I **really** couldn't stand Robbie. And it burned me
that Wendy would even talk to a guy like that.
So I knew then and there that I had to do whatever
it took to keep him away from Wendy.
Luckily, I had my sister, who would help me.

Right, Mabel?

Right? Mabel?

OH MY GOSH A PIG!
There he was, at Farmer Sprott's
booth! This pig—you wouldn't
believe how cute he was!
And all you had to do was
guess the pig's weight and
you could take him home!

So I knew then and there that I had to do whatever it took
to GET THAT PIG. I walked right over, and the pig said,
"Mabel!" or "doorbell." Either way, WOW! The farmer said the
pig just made a pig noise, but what do farmers know?

I guessed that the pig weighed fifteen pounds,
because the farmer called the pig Ol' Fifteen Pound-y.
SO I WAS THE PROUD OWNER OF A PIG!!!

I was thrown over for a pig.

But I could do this! I found Wendy, and we walked around the Mystery Fair. We came across one of those games where you throw the ball and knock over the cans to win a prize. Wendy wanted a stuffed animal that was either a duck or a panda. It was hard to tell. But if **she** wanted one, I was going to **win it!**

I put my money down and threw a ball right at the cans. And do you know what happened?

The ball **bounced** off the cans and hit Wendy in the eye.

Of all the **terrible** luck! I had to make this better, fast!

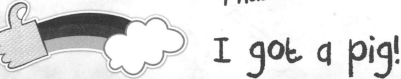

I got a pig!

Then I remembered that Grunkle Stan had an ice machine in front of the Mystery Shack. Unlike most of the things at the Mystery Shack, the ice machine actually worked. So I picked up a bag and ran back toward Wendy so I could put the ice on her eye.

That was what I was trying to do, anyway, when I crashed right into this weird guy who came out of nowhere! The ice went all over the place, and I told the guy to watch where he was going.

He didn't say anything at all.
He just ran away. Weird.

 I still have a pig!

I picked up the ice and put it back in the bag. But when I got back, I saw that Robbie was already there! Even **WORSE**, they were hanging out by the freezy cone stand! Robbie had bought a freezy cone and was holding it up to Wendy's eye to reduce the swelling.

Then things got even worse.
I heard . . .

The same thing she had said to me!

Did I mention that I had **a pig**? I was so excited I ran to Dipper and showed him **Waddles**! See, I named my pig Waddles because he **waddles**! **Ha ha!** Great name, right?

Dipper seemed down, though. I told him that just because I had Waddles in my life, it didn't mean that I would love Dipper any less. Well, maybe a **little** less.

Then I saw what Dipper was **REALLY** bummed about. Wendy and Robbie were heading into the Tunnel of Love and corndogs. **Together!**

I couldn't let this happen to my brother. So Dr. Waddles was on the case! That's what I called Waddles after I dressed him up like a doctor. I said, "We've got a boy in here with a broken heart!" Ha! The jokes were golden! I KNEW that was what Dipper needed, because laughter is the best medicine after actual medicine.

But Dipper didn't laugh. Was I not funny? No, that couldn't possibly be the case. He must REALLY be upset!

Well, yeah, I was upset. I had just ruined everything with Wendy forever. FOREVER. I just . . . I just wished that I could go back and undo my mistake. I asked Mabel if she ever felt that way.

She said . . .
Nope! I do everything right all the time!

Wendy only went out with Robbie because he happened to be there with the freezy cone, and she only NEEDED the freezy cone because of the ball hitting her in the face, and I would have had the ice instead of Robbie if it hadn't been for—

—that guy! The one with the tool belt!
He ruined my life!

That's right, Dipper, he did! Not only that, but he was talking craZy talk! He was fiddling with this watch he was wearing, babbling about activating "stealth mode." His clothes started changing colors, but we could still totally see him. Then he took out this weird red screwdriver thingy and started to make adjustments to the watch.

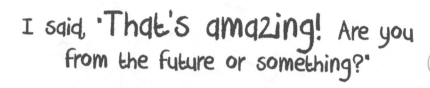

I said, 'That's amazing! Are you from the future or something?"

The guy panicked and threw a wipe at me and said, 'Memory wipe!'

But it was just a baby wipe.

Then things got a little stranger. The guy said that he was a time traveler named Blendin Blandin, and that he was part of the Time Anomaly Removal Crew. He even said he had a time machine.

That got me thinking. Maybe I could borrow the time machine and use it to set everything right with Wendy!

The time traveler said that it was out of the question, though. Something about the time machine being sensitive and complicated.

It looked like a tape measure.

Then he did something to the tape measure, and the time traveler disappeared in a FLASH! When he reappeared a second later, he was dressed like a fancy king! Dipper and I thought maybe he had traveled back to medieval times, but he had just traveled back fifteen years, to when there used to be a costume store where the Mystery Shack stood.

Blendin told us that his superiors sent him back to our time because some time anomalies were scheduled to happen **right here!** But he was really tired. Maybe it's because we're twins, but Mabel and I came up with the same plan at the same time. We convinced Blendin that he could use a break from his job and should go on one of the Mystery Fair rides.

He agreed! When he got on the Rusty Barrel ride, Soos told Blendin that he had to remove his tool belt, because one of the tools might fly off and accidentally fix something. Blendin took it off, and I grabbed the time machine!

We went back to the Mystery Shack and used the time machine to travel to the past—six hours in the past! That way, Dipper could make sure he never hit Wendy in the eye with the ball, and everything would be glorious!

NOW

SIX HOURS EARLIER

Here was my chance to do it over **again**! But when I played the game, Wendy got hit with the ball again! So I figured maybe if we traveled back in time **once** more, I could make it work. Mabel and I used the time machine again, and I returned to the same spot with Wendy. And guess what happened **this** time?

I STILL hit Wendy with the ball!

I couldn't figure out what was going wrong! Then I realized that I needed help.

I needed Mabel!

She could help me fix it so that Wendy wouldn't get hit!

But how was I going to win Waddles all over again if I was helping Dipper instead? Dipper said it would only take a few minutes. And he was **my brother**, and didn't he deserve a chance to be as happy as me and Waddles would be in the future?

The answer to that question is YES, silly! When Dipper threw the ball, it sailed clear over the stand, rolled off a tent, then bounced off the Mystery Dog stand. The ball would have gone straight into the woods if I hadn't popped up and redirected it using a piece of rain gutter.

The ball bounced right off the lever of Grunkle Stan's dunk tank, and no, he didn't go in. The ball came back, knocked the top of Robbie's freezy cone onto the ground, then ricocheted into the cans, knocking them down! I won! And Wendy didn't get hit in the eye!

Robbie came over and was about to ask Wendy on a date. But Wendy was so happy with the stuffed animal she won she didn't even care about him. Our plan worked!

It only SORT of worked! When I went over to Farmer Sprott's booth, someone ELSE had won Waddles! I did the only thing a person in my position could do. I screamed!

And I did. Not. Stop. SCREAMING!

Until I did!

We had messed up the time line! I couldn't live without Waddles. I knew we had to go back and fix things. Except Dipper didn't want to, because he had already GOTTEN what he wanted!

I'd worked so hard to fix it so I didn't hit Wendy in the eye and she'd want to hang out with me instead of Robbie. I **couldn't** risk losing that! So Mabel and I fought over the time machine.

And we started traveling through time!

First we went back **150 years** to pioneer times, which wasn't great. Then we went back to prehistoric times, which was even less great, but more dinosaur-y.

We almost got eaten by a T. rex!

Then we traveled back to the present, except it was **two weeks** earlier! We saw the old man at Lake Gravity Falls, screaming, "I seen it! I seen it again!" I think it might have been that Gravity Falls Gobblewonker guy. Anyway . . .

We kept on jumping through time, back and forth, and I don't know about Dipper, but I was feeling kind of sick! Like I had eaten a whole bunch of Smile Dip, which I'd sworn **never** to eat again!

We argued so much, and all I thought about was what I wanted. I didn't really stop to think **how much** Waddles meant to Mabel. We traveled into the future, and I saw what would happen if Mabel wasn't able to be with her pig. **She would be so unhappy!**

I couldn't live with myself if that happened.

So we went back to the past, and I threw the ball and hit Wendy in the eye. Mabel won Waddles.

Dipper had given up so much for me and Waddles to be together. I loved Dipper so much I could have hugged him forever!

Waddles wanted to hug him, too! There was just so much hugging!

I'm FUZZY!

MYSTERY DOGS

Some might argue there was too MUCH hugging.

NOT POSSIBLE!

Then the Time Paradox Avoidance Enforcement Squadron arrived to punish Blendin for violations of the Time Travelers' Code of Conduct! Blendin **swore** he'd get revenge on me and Mabel by making sure our parents would never meet. But the Time Cops took him away, and nothing happened, so I guess Blendin forgot.

Mabel even made things right with Wendy! Robbie was walking with her, eating a candy apple. Mabel let Waddles go, and he went right for the candy apple!
Robbie **freaked out**, flung the apple, and backed up into a tub of hot water that **shrank** his new jeans!

Wendy wasn't going out with Robbie anymore!

I guess everything did work out after all.
Even if we did sort of mess with the time line.

How could I ever thank Mabel?

How could you ever thank Mabel? You could start by letting us give you another hug! Who loves hugs? Dipper loves hugs! Who loves giving hugs? Mabel and Waddles!

The end!

But not of hugs! Hugs are FOREVER!

"WELCOME TO THE MYSTERY FAIR!"

THAT'S WHAT I SAID! MAYBE! I THINK I DID. SEEMS LIKE SOMETHING A GUY THROWING A MYSTERY FAIR SHOULD SAY. ANYWAY, I HAD THIS GREAT RACKET GOING WITH THE DUNK TANK. SOOS FIXED IT SO THE LEVER DIDN'T WORK. IT WAS IMPOSSIBLE TO KNOCK ME INTO THE TANK! SO PEOPLE WOULD SHOW UP, PAY THEIR MONEY, AND TRY TO KNOCK ME IN.

BUT THEY COULDN'T?

THEY GOT SO MAD.

THAT'S WHEN I STARTED WITH THE TEASING. TEASING IS A GREAT WAY OF SAYING, "I'M BETTER THAN YOU, WHY DON'T YOU GIVE UP? OH, THAT'S RIGHT, YOUR EGO WON'T ALLOW IT?" THEN THEY PAY MORE MONEY TO TRY TO KNOCK ME OFF.

I'M **NOT** SAYING IT'S THE WORLD'S MOST BRILLIANT PLAN, BUT I CHALLENGE YOU TO NAME ANOTHER ONE.

THE DAY HAD BEEN **GREAT** SO FAR. I COULDN'T WAIT TO SEE HOW MUCH MONEY WE HAD. MAYBE I SHOULD HAVE QUIT WHILE I WAS AHEAD, BUT THAT'S NEVER BEEN MY STYLE, MOSTLY BECAUSE I'M NEVER AHEAD.

ALONG COMES THIS GUY WITH THESE BIG ARMS AND FANCY CLOTHES, SO I YELLED, "HEY! BICEPS! YEAH, I'M TALKING TO YOU, HAIRCUT?"

BECAUSE HE HAD A HAIRCUT.

THE GUY WALKED OVER AND LOOKED AT ME, AND I TOLD HIM TO TAKE HIS BEST SHOT!

SO HE DID.

WITH SOME KINDA FANCY SPACE GUN.

BLASTED THE HANDLE RIGHT OFF THE DUNK TANK, AND INTO THE WATER I WENT.

MAN, I **HATE** THE MYSTERY FAIR.

THE END, AND GOOD RIDDANCE.

SUMMERWEEN

You know the old saying "You learn something new every day"? Before I came to Gravity Falls, I would have told you that was a big lie. There were days when I thought I hadn't learned ANYTHING. But when you hang around Grunkle Stan, you're constantly learning new things.

Take **Summerween**, for example.

Summerween!

The beautiful marriage of **Summer** and **Halloween!** Grunkle Stan explained that the people of Gravity Falls loved Halloween so much they decided to celebrate it two days a year. And as it just so happens, lucky for us, the first of them was today.

Our first stop was the party supply store, because Grunkle Stan needed to get an industrial-sized barrel full of fake blood.

Do you really think that was **necessary?**

Oh, Dipper! OF COURSE it was necessary.

SUMMERWEEN SUPERSTORE

Why WOULDN'T you need an industrial-sized barrel full of fake blood?

Have I mentioned how excited I was?

I was SO excited. As soon as we got home, we went straight to work. I just knew that we were going to have the best costumes! And having the best costumes meant getting the most candy. And getting the most CANDY meant having the biggest stomachaches ever!

YES! I have to admit I was really excited, too. Back home, Mabel and I were kind of known as the kings of trick-or-treating. That's because we're twins. Twins in costumes. It turns out that people really love seeing twins in costumes!

One year we went as a pair of black cats. Another time, we were salt and pepper shakers.

OOOH!
And zombies!

But before we could get too excited, Soos told us about
the Summerween Trickster.

According to him, the Summerween Trickster was a ghoulish figure who went door to door each Summerween, looking for children who lacked the Summerween spirit.

Actually, Soos said that the Summerween Trickster would EAT children who lacked the Summerween spirit.

Creepy if true!
But Mabel and I wouldn't have to worry. I mean, who could possibly have MORE Summerween spirit than us?

Then the doorbell rang. The first trick-or-treaters of Summerween! Grunkle Stan told us to hand out a bowl of really awful candy. With names like Sand Pop, Gummy Chairs, and Mr. Adequate-bar, you can imagine how not good they were.

Anyway, when I answered the door, I expected to hear screams of "Trick or treat!" Instead, it was Wendy! And Robbie! I was so embarrassed. I mean, not like I liked Wendy or anything.

Of course not! Why even mention it?

Exactly! But I was a little self-conscious. Mabel was busy with Soos when Robbie asked if we were going trick-or-treating. But before I could say anything, Wendy said . . .

OF COURSE he's not going trick-or-treating.

I didn't know what to say. I didn't want to look like a baby. Then Wendy invited me to a party at her friend's house, and she left.

What was I going to do?
What was I going to say to Mabel?

And speaking of Mabel
(THAT'S ME!),
I was introducing my friends
Candy and Grenda to Grunkle Stan.
They had amazing costumes!
Candy was dressed as, well, candy,
and Grenda was a witch. As for me?
I was jelly! Because Dipper was going to be peanut butter!

Right, Dipper?
    Uh . . .
        I said, "RIGHT, DIPPER?"

I couldn't do it.

Wear a costume, I mean. If Wendy saw me wearing a costume,
then she'd think I really WAS a little kid. And I couldn't
have that. So I sort of fake coughed some. I told Mabel
that I was sick and that she should just go on without me.

Well, I wasn't having it! Dipper needed to fight through it!
This was Summerween! The best night of the year!
And I wasn't seeing a lot of Summerween spirit
coming from that guy!

Someone knocked on the door, and I was glad for the interruption. At least I wouldn't have to explain to Mabel why I didn't want to go trick-or-treating.
When I opened the door, there was a big guy wearing a tiny little mask and holding a candy bag. He said . . .

Trick or treat!

But he looked so big! So I said, "You're a little old for this, man. Sorry." I didn't give him any of Grunkle Stan's horrible candy, and I closed the door.

That was not in the spirit of Summerween! Dipper said that he just wasn't "feeling it" tonight. Well, I had just the cure for that! Trick-or-treating! WOOO!

Then there was **another** knock at the door. Dipper opened it, and it was the same guy from before. Dipper told him to just go to another house.
But I was like, where's your Summerween hospitality? So I apologized for Dipper.

Well, apparently an apology wasn't going to do it. Because it wasn't somebody who was too old for trick-or-treating. It was . . .

the Summerween Trickster!

I was literally just about to say that.

sorry!

Anyway, the Summerween Trickster said that I had insulted him and that we must pay with our lives. Then he devoured a kid dressed like a pirate. So, you know, traumatizing. The Trickster said the only way to avoid that fate was to bring him a treat: **five hundred pieces of candy** delivered before the last jack-o'-melon went out.

Five hundred pieces? That was impossible!
And what was a jack-o'-melon? I was guessing it was like a jack-o'-lantern except instead of a pumpkin it was a melon? The one he had looked like a watermelon.
THAT wasn't a thing back home.

It was settled!

Dipper was coming with us whether he was sick or not! We brought a wheelbarrow with us, because we were going to need it to carry the five hundred pieces of candy we were sure to get. Dipper wondered why we couldn't just buy the candy to appease the Summerween Trickster, but I told him that would take the fun out of trick-or-treat or die.

Trick or treat!

On one of our first stops, there was a woman dressed like a ball of yarn, and she was covered in cats. They were SO CUTE! I could have stayed there playing with the cats all night. But we couldn't! Because we needed candy!

The woman guessed what each of the others was dressed as, and she mostly got it wrong. By "mostly," I mean "entirely." Then she asked me what I was supposed to be. I told her that I wasn't dressed as anything, and that we were in kind of a hurry. So guess what? She gave each person who dressed up only ONE PIECE OF CANDY! Someone even got a circus peanut. A circus peanut! You know—loser candy!

At this rate, we'd never make the Summerween Trickster's goal and we'd be devoured for sure. If we were gonna pull this off, Dipper was gonna have to up his game. No matter how much he protested, if we were going to live, he was gonna HAVE to dress up!

Not being alive anymore is a pretty compelling argument, so I decided to dress up after all. I put on my peanut butter costume, and Mabel was dressed as jelly. I was so embarrassed. What if we ran into Wendy? And Robbie? He'd just make fun of me!

Worry not, Brother!

When we trick-or-treated at the next house, our costumes went over BIG-TIME! The guy who answered the door was moved to tears by our twins tap-dance routine, complete with jazz hands. He dumped a whole bowl of candy into our bags!

Every house we went to, Dipper and I pulled the twins act. We gave 'em the dancing, the big, wide eyes, and jazz hands— so many jazz hands! The people couldn't resist. Before we knew it, we had **exactly** four hundred ninety-nine pieces of candy. All we needed was one more piece and we'd be spared from spending the rest of eternity in the stomach of the Summerween Trickster! That's assuming he didn't digest us.

Everyone but me ran off to the last house. Then Wendy and Robbie pulled up in a van. I couldn't let them see me in my costume! So I took it off and ditched it behind a bush, along with the wheelbarrow of candy. Wendy asked me if I would be at the party.

I said, "Definitely!"

Whoa, whoa, whoa. Dipper was going to a party?

So THAT was why he had been acting so weird all night! Dipper wasn't even sick. He just wanted to go to the party with Wendy, and he was gonna ditch me to do it!

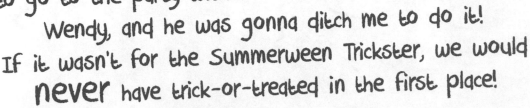

If it wasn't for the Summerween Trickster, we would **never** have trick-or-treated in the first place!

Mabel was pretty mad at me because I lied to her about the whole "I'm too sick to go trick-or-treating" thing. And she was also angry because she didn't see the candy anywhere. But I told her everything was okay because I stashed the candy behind a bush. At least, I thought I had. It turned out the wheelbarrow had **rolled down a hill** and **dumped** the candy into a stream.

Most of the candy had already floated away!

Maybe there would have been time to get more candy, but the last jack-o'-melon had already gone out! And standing **right in front of** us was the Summerween Trickster. In a really creepy voice, he said . . .

So, children . . . where's my candy?

I tried to explain that we'd had all five hundred pieces of candy but it had rolled down the hill and was now floating in the stream. I told him that we could still get it!

Except he said that it was too late! It was going to take some pretty quick thinking to get us out of this one!

I threw a Blorch candy bar at his face.

And we ran!

The Summerween Trickster was really fast, though. He caught right up to us and tried to grab us with his four arms. Well, he didn't try so much as he actually DID grab us. I was sure the monster was going to open his massive jaw and drop us into his mouth when Soos suddenly drove his truck right through the creature!

Dipper thought it was all over. But it wasn't. I mean, I was really mad at him! Trying to ditch me like that. Oh, and also, the Summerween Trickster was still alive. The monster jumped on top of Soos's truck. The creature fell off, but Soos was kind of all riled up from that, and he accidentally drove smack into the party supply store!

The Summerween Trickster was blocking the exit. The only way out of the store was past him! Mabel wondered why I was suddenly so worried about the monster when all I had cared about before was Wendy. But it wasn't true. I just thought . . . well, that maybe I was getting a little too old for trick-or-treating. Mabel said that was why we HAD to go trick-or-treating: because it wasn't long until we'd be too old.

We needed to find some way to disguise ourselves so the Summerween Trickster wouldn't notice us. Luckily, we had crashed into the party store. We put on masks and stayed still. When the monster walked by, he didn't even see us!

We ran for the door! And we might have even made it, too, if it wasn't for . . . Well, I don't want to point fingers, but Soos was COMPLETELY responsible.

There were all these little creepy cackling skull decorations, and Soos just HAD to press the button on one of them.
The skull started laughing, and the Summerween Trickster raced over to us!

He ate Soos first, which I guess was appropriate? But then the Summerween Trickster was going to eat us!

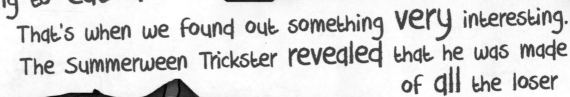

That's when we found out something VERY interesting. The Summerween Trickster revealed that he was made of all the loser candy the kids from Gravity Falls threw away!

What happened next is . . . Well, I'm not really sure what happened next. Soos burst out of the Summerween Trickster's candy body and started to eat.

That's right: he was **eating** all that loser candy! Black licorice, circus peanuts, even those bars of chocolate with that white powder stuff on them, whatever that is—Soos was eating it all!

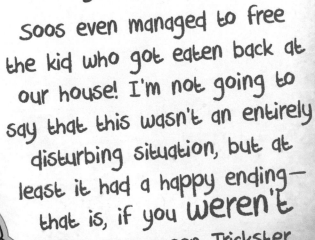

Soos even managed to free the kid who got eaten back at our house! I'm not going to say that this wasn't an entirely disturbing situation, but at least it had a happy ending— that is, if you **weren't** the Summerween Trickster.

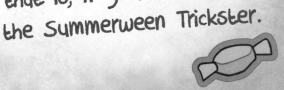

When we got back to the Mystery Shack, I couldn't believe what I saw. Wendy was there, carving a jack-o'-melon! She said that the party was pretty lame and that Robbie had to go home sick. So she came here. I told her that we went trick-or-treating, and she didn't think that was babyish at all.

The night was turning out okay after all! Except after all that trick-or-treating, we didn't even have **any** good candy!

Or so we thought! Grunkle Stan pulled out some huge bags of Summerween candy but didn't say where he had gotten it. Oh well! For the rest of the night, we watched the Summerween Movie Marathon on TV—hours and hours of nonstop horror movies!

And we ate candy. Sweet, delicious candy.

The end!

I KNOW, I KNOW. RIGHT ABOUT NOW, YOU'RE PROBABLY WONDERING, "WHERE DID HE GET ALL THAT CANDY? THE GOOD STUFF, NOT THAT LOSER CANDY HE PAWNED OFF ON ALL THE TRICK-OR-TREATERS." GOOD QUESTION! Y'SEE, EVERY SUMMERWEEN, I LIKE TO SCARE THE PANTS OFF ANYONE WHO RINGS THE DOORBELL ASKING FOR CANDY.

BUT THE PANTS-SCARING-OFF WASN'T GOING SO WELL THIS YEAR. THE FIRST GROUP OF KIDS WASN'T EVEN REMOTELY FRIGHTENED WHEN I JUMPED OUT AT THEM FROM THE SHADOWS. THEY DIDN'T EVEN REACT WHEN MY FACE MELTED OFF! DON'T WORRY, IT DIDN'T REALLY MELT OFF. NOT THAT YOU WOULD EVEN WORRY.

KIDS ARE TOO INTO THEMSELVES THESE DAYS!

ANYWAY, I KNEW IF I WAS GONNA SCARE 'EM, I'D NEED ANOTHER PLAN.

I HAD THIS GREAT IDEA FOR A SCARE, AND I THOUGHT MABEL'S PIG, WADDLES, COULD HELP—WHETHER HE WANTED TO OR NOT? THE KIDS WAITED OUTSIDE WHILE I GOT READY. WHEN I RETURNED, I SUCKERED 'EM IN BY SAYING STUFF LIKE "ALL RIGHT, YOU GOT ME, KIDS," AND "YOU GUYS WIN." Ha! THEN I PULLED MY GAG ON 'EM. WADDLES BURST OUT OF A FAKE CHEST I WAS WEARING, MADE TO LOOK LIKE MY REAL CHEST!

THAT WOULDA SCARED ANYONE!

EXCEPT IT DIDN'T!

RIGHT THEN, I KNEW WHAT SHAME FELT LIKE. I DECIDED TO TAKE A BATH AND WASH IT OFF—THE SHAME, I MEAN. BUT BEFORE I COULD GET IN THE TUB, I HEARD SOMEONE IN THE HOUSE. IT WAS THOSE KIDS, LOOKING FOR CANDY! I GUESS THEY'D NEVER SEEN AN OLD GUY WEARING BOXERS AND A SHOWER CAP BEFORE, SO THEY TOTALLY LOST IT.

TALK ABOUT SCREAMING IN FEAR! THEY RAN AWAY AND NEVER CAME BACK. THEY EVEN LEFT THEIR SUMMERWEEN CANDY!

I GUESS I'VE STILL GOT IT!

THE END!

DREAMSCAPERERS

Every once in a while, you just have to press the "pause" button on life and play a nice, relaxing game. And every once in a while, that nice, relaxing game is going to be interrupted by Grunkle Stan screaming,

"Kids! Come quick! I need you to laugh at this with me!"

Life can't all be fun and games! Sometimes it has to be fun and games and even MORE fun! So we ran downstairs into the living room and saw Grunkle Stan watching TV. There was Gideon, Grunkle Stan's archnemesis! Gideon was a self-described "child psychic."

You mean "fraud."

Right! Anyway, Grunkle Stan was making fun of Gideon's commercial. Gideon was always trying to trick Grunkle into losing the Mystery Shack.

Gideon really was **pretty obnoxious.** And **evil.**
Nobody in the Mystery Shack liked him. Wendy said she
caught him stealing her moisturizer one time. And Soos,
who doesn't seem to dislike anyone, said that it was our
mutual hatred of Gideon that bonded us together.
I'm not sure if that was true, but it was hard
to deny our **intense loathing** of Gideon.

While we were all laughing, there was a
disturbing detail in Gideon's commercial
that had me on edge.

OH! Was it the part where
the commercial said, "Come
on down to Lil' Gideon's
Tent o' Telepathy, opening
soon at THIS location"?
And then they showed a
picture of Gideon's Tent of Telepathy
crashing down on top of the Mystery Shack, implying
that he was going to open up shop right on this very spot?

Uh, yeah, I think it was that part.

Grunkle Stan didn't seem to be too concerned. He said the only way that Gideon could get the Mystery Shack was if he broke into his safe and stole the deed—which is **exactly** what Gideon was doing.

Somehow he had weaseled his way into Grunkle Stan's office and was trying to crack the safe to get the deed to the Mystery Shack! Gideon made it out like he was playing some kind of three-dimensional chess game. Y'know, saying stuff like "We seem to have entered a dangerous game of cat and mouse. But the question remains, who is the cat, and who is the—"

Too bad for Gideon that Grunkle Stan has exactly no patience whatsoever. He told Soos to get the broom, and Gideon panicked! "Oh, no! Not the broom!" he said. It was hilarious! Grunkle Stan chased Gideon **with the broom** out of his office and right onto the porch.

But Gideon delivered an **ominous** warning. "You mark my words, Stanford! One day I'm gonna get that combination, and once I steal that deed, you'll never see the Mystery Shack again . . . again . . . again . . . again!"
Why are you doing that?
Repeating "again" over and over?
You know—it's like an echo!

Gideon was gone, and that was the end of that. **Or so we thought!** But before we get to that part, I have to mention that while we were trying to watch a movie, Soos ran into the living room, **frightened** out of his wits.

Dudes! There's a bat in the kitchen!

Grunkle Stan told us not to worry, that he had **everything** under control.

Then he told **ME** to take care of it.

I was so tired of it! Every time there was some kind of horrible job that needed to be done, Grunkle Stan told ME to do it. Not Mabel, not Wendy, not Soos— ME. I asked Soos why that was, and all he said was that Grunkle Stan's personality was one of "life's great mysteries." Then he said something about trying to lick your own elbow.

I bet you CAN'T lick your own elbow!

Sigh.

Just when I thought it couldn't get worse than shooing bats out of the house, Grunkle Stan told me to unclog the sink.

It was never-ending with this guy!

Speaking of Gideon—

I wasn't speaking of Gideon, I was—

SPEAKING OF GIDEON,

unbeknownst to all of us, at that very moment, Gideon was in the forest, reading from the mysterious Journal #2! He started to recite cryptic words that would

invite uncontrollable terror!

We didn't know
that then.

Relax, Dipper, it's called
FORESHADOWING.

While Dipper had to stay inside doing every conceivable type of chore, Soos and I went outside, because I wanted to see him lick his own elbow.

Y'know, because where ELSE are you going to go to watch someone lick their elbow?

Anyway, Soos and I stumbled on Gideon chanting words from that book, like I said, and suddenly, this strange triangle-shaped guy appeared out of nowhere!

He said his name was Bill.

Gideon said, "Listen to me, demon! I have a job for you. I need you to enter the mind of Stanford Pines and steal the code to his safe!" And wouldn't you know it, this Bill guy agreed to do it! He said that in return, Gideon would need to help him with something.

Then Bill disappeared after saying that Grunkle Stan had just fallen asleep and that he was going to invade his mind. We had to warn Grunkle Stan!

Soos and I raced back to the Mystery Shack and found Grunkle Stan asleep in a chair in the living room. Dipper was there, and Soos told him about the evil triangle guy and how he was gonna break into Grunkle Stan's mind to steal the combination to his safe!

Evil triangle guy? That sounded familiar! I reached for the journal I'd found, and flipped to a page that matched Soos and Mabel's description.
The book said:

> Beware Bill . . . the most powerful and dangerous creature I've ever encountered. Whatever you do, NEVER let him into your mind.

Then we saw the shadow of a triangle appear on the wall behind Grunkle Stan. Grunkle's eyes opened and started to glow!
And he moaned!

The book said it is possible to follow the demon into a person's mind and prevent his chaos. One must simply recite this incantation.

I know I should have been all gung ho, like, "Let's go get that demon!" but I wasn't. Truthfully?

I was angry!

I had spent all day cleaning sinks and getting rid of bats for Grunkle Stan, and now I was going to have to save him from some weird brain demon, too?

But if we DIDN'T go after the demon, then Gideon would get the combination to Grunkle's safe, and then he'd get the Mystery Shack, and also,

WEIRD BRAIN DEMON! Sigh.

So it looked like we were about to go on a journey into the most horrifying, disturbing place any of us had ever been: Grunkle Stan's mind!

We recited the incantation and woke up **inside** our grunkle's mind! It was really foggy, and at first it was hard to see anything. But then I could see the Mystery Shack, but it was kind of **twisted** and **different**. There were extra doors and upside-down signs, and **WOW!** So **THAT** was what the inside of Grunkle Stan's mind looked like.

I had to be careful not to get too distracted, though. We had to be on the lookout for that triangle guy.

Aaaaaand that's **exactly** when Bill appeared above us and said . . .

Yeah, look out for the triangle guy!

I dove at him, saying,
"You leave our uncle's brain alone, you isosceles monster!"
But I just passed right **into** him!
Then, a second later, I flew out of him and hit the ground.

I asked Bill what he wanted with Grunkle Stan's mind, anyway. He said that he was looking for the code to his safe. He told us that inside the Mystery Shack in Grunkle's brain was a hall of memories with a **thousand doors**—each one representing a different memory.

Behind one of those doors was a memory of Grunkle Stan inputting the code. Now all Bill had to do was find the right door, **grab the code,** and **give it to Gideon!**

I told Bill that we were gonna stop him! But he disappeared before we could do **anything.** Now we were going to have to **find him and stop him!**

We raced into the hall of memories and started opening door after door. While we didn't find the door that had the combination to Grunkle Stan's safe, we DID find that he had lots of weird memories. I was kind of **sorry that we looked!**

There were **SO MANY** doors it didn't seem like we could possibly check them all. But then I realized that if we wanted to find something in Grunkle Stan's memory, we were gonna have to **THINK** like him. He was always hiding stuff, right?

Then Soos reminded us that Grunkle always hid stuff under the rug in the gift shop.

Mabel had the right idea!

We checked under the rug and saw a door. Inside was Grunkle Stan's memory of the time he put the new code into his safe! Now all we had to do was **destroy** the door so Bill couldn't find it.

Except we had done the **exact opposite.** In trying to find the code first, we had **led Bill right to it!**

Bill snatched the door with the combination, then disappeared. So I took off after him! Soon I found him and Gideon. Bill was just about to give the combination to that little creep when I fired a suction cup dart at the door from my trusty dart gun, which I just happened to have with me in this **strange** dreamlike world inside Grunkle Stan's mind!

The door **flew** out of Bill's hand and into a pit of forgotten memories. Anything that fell into the pit was instantly forgotten— **forever!** And so this memory was!

Grunkle Stan's secret was completely safe!

And now Bill was **completely** angry! He said, "You can't even imagine what you just cost me! Do you have any idea what I'm like when I'm mad?"

And I didn't, because I'd only just met him. Like, how could I?

Bill was going to do something **terrible** to Mabel and Soos if I didn't act fast. Luckily, I ran into Grunkle Stan himself! Or his mind. Or . . . something. It's kind of confusing if you stop to think about it, which I don't recommend doing. Anyway, he said that because it was HIS mind, I could do **anything** I wanted to.

So I decided that I had **laser vision**—and I used it to **blast Bill!**

Bill was actually scared!
If we could conjure anything we wanted in Grunkle Stan's mindscape, then we could defeat him! I could even give myself **kittens for fists**, because what's cuter than kitten fists? What's that? Nothing?

YOU'RE RIGHT!

Bill was fighting mad.

He blasted at us, but I said, "Hamster-ball shields, activate!" So we did it! The beam from Bill's eye hit our hamster balls, which were pink, because best color. And the beam reflected back at Bill, and he **screamed in pain!** It was so neat!

Finally, Bill said, **"No, no, enough!"** He claimed that he was impressed by us and that we were more clever than we looked. He decided he was going to let us off the hook for now because we might come in handy later. And then he said something **really creepy** that I'll never forget....

We'd done it: the three of us had saved Grunkle Stan's secret and the Mystery Shack and defeated Bill!

And we got to have kitten fists!

Yes, and kitten fists.

Anyway, we'd beaten Bill, and now all that remained was to leave Grunkle Stan's mind and return to the real world. But how were we going to do that? Before we could figure that out, we started to disappear. It must have been because Grunkle Stan was waking up!

Suddenly, we found ourselves back in the Mystery Shack. We were all in the living room, just like we had been before we entered Grunkle Stan's mind! While Dipper, Soos, and I remembered **everything** from our epic and incredibly weird journey into Grunkle's mind, he didn't seem to know **anything** about it. He wanted to know what we were all doing there!

I was just glad to be back, and really happy that Grunkle Stan was okay—even if he did make me clean sinks and chase after bats. I threw my arms around him, and Grunkle Stan thought I was trying to hug him. But it wasn't a hug—it was a choke hold!

Then Grunkle Stan said the words I never thought I'd hear. He said, "Not bad, kid. Not bad."

It was **almost** perfect.
Except I didn't get to keep the **kitten fists.**

We can't have everything, Mabel.

The end!

OKAY, LOOK, YOU'RE PROBABLY SAYING TO YOURSELF, "HEY! STAN PINES! JERKFACE! WHY ARE YOU ALWAYS MAKIN' THE KID CLEAN UP SINKS AND SHOO BATS OUT OF THE KITCHEN?" WELL, THE FIRST THING I'LL SAY IS, MIND YOUR OWN BUSINESS. SERIOUSLY. DON'T YOU HAVE ANYTHING BETTER TO DO? MAYBE GO TO SLEEP? LIKE, RIGHT NOW?

SECOND, I'M KINDA HARD ON DIPPER BECAUSE . . . BECAUSE HE REMINDS ME OF MYSELF WHEN I WAS A KID. EVERYONE USED TO PICK ON ME.

AND I HAD TO TOUGHEN UP SO WHEN THE WORLD FOUGHT, I COULD FIGHT BACK. AN' I JUST WANT THE SAME FOR HIM.

SO SURE, I MAKE HIM UNCLOG SINKS!

SURE, I MAKE HIM GET RID OF BATS!

SURE, I MAKE HIM SLICE LOGS!

THAT LAST ONE'S ACTUALLY JUST BECAUSE WHO DOESN'T LIKE WATCHING SOMEONE SLICE LOGS? IT'S RELAXING.

ANYWAY. POINT IS THE KID HAS THE STUFF, AND . . . AND, WELL, I'M ACTUALLY PROUD OF HIM. BUT DON'T EVER TELL HIM I SAID THAT. HIS HEAD'S BIG ENOUGH AS IT IS.

I MEAN, PHYSICALLY, HIS HEAD IS HUGE. IT'S LIKE A HAM.

THE END,

NOW GET OUTTA MY HOUSE.

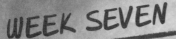

GIDEON RISES

There I was, sound asleep, when suddenly I woke up with a start!

I'd just had the **worst possible dream ever.** Gideon had stolen the deed to the Mystery Shack after all! Then he kicked us out and destroyed the shack. And then we all had to move in with Soos's grandma!

That would be the worst possible dream ever, except that it wasn't a dream! That's EXACTLY what happened! Gideon DID get the deed to the Mystery Shack. When his scheme to have Bill steal the deed didn't work, Gideon resorted to good old-fashioned dynamite. He blew the safe and took the deed. Then Gideon told us we had to leave, and he started to demolish the Mystery Shack!

So there we were, kicked out of our own home. We turned on the news, and sure enough, their top story was Gideon! "Child psychic Gideon Gleeful has taken surprise ownership of the Mystery Shack," the news report said.

The reporter asked Gideon exactly what he was planning to do. Gideon said, "I have a BIG announcement to make today, and I'd like to cordially invite all the good people of Gravity Falls to join me. Free admission to everyone who wears their Gideon pins!"

Gideon held up a pin and winked at the camera. It was gross.

I felt **terrible**, like it was somehow all
my *fault* that Gideon had gotten the deed.

Well, you have to look at the bright side, Dipper!
Now we were living with Soos!
In his living room! While he
sat in his underwear!
Playing with his racetrack!

Yeah, when you put it like that, it
still doesn't sound great.
Also, the race cars were out of batteries, so the
only way we could play with that racetrack was if we
pretended. And I didn't have time for pretend. There
was too much reality that needed to be dealt with.

For instance, Soos **coughed,** and a couple
pieces of cereal came out and landed on his
chest. Then he picked them up, put them back
in **his mouth,** and ate them. **Again.**

"We've gotta get the shack
back," Grunkle Stan said.

We just had to find out what Gideon had planned. So me, Mabel, Soos, and Grunkle Stan put on some disguises and headed over to the Mystery Shack. When we got there, we saw a big sign that said MYSTERY SHACK GRAND CLOSING! Then Gideon jumped through a big paper Gideon face, and the crowd—yeah, that's right, there was a crowd—went wild.

MYSTERY SHACK GRAND CLOSING!

Hello, Gravity Falls! It's me, your favorite child psychic!

Well, he wasn't MY favorite child psychic.

He wasn't mine, either! In fact, I'm pretty sure I don't even HAVE a favorite child psychic.

As we moved through the crowd, we heard people talking about Gideon and how amazing he was. How he seemed to know their secrets. One lady was shocked that Gideon guessed the secret ingredient in her coffee omelet! (I wanna say it was coffee.)

We got closer to the stage, and Gideon stood
behind a podium, talking into a microphone.
He raised his hands for quiet. Then he said,
"Ladies and gentlemen! I am delighted to
announce my new plans for the former
Mystery Shack. I give you . . .

"Gideonland!"

Come on, Mabel! I was telling the story!

You stopped. I thought you were done.

No, I only paused for dramatic effect! Anyway,
he said, "Gideonland! We're gonna turn
this dirty ol' shack into three square miles of

Gideon-tertainment!"

But that wasn't the WORST OF it! The crowd was going nuts as Gideon made another announcement.

And introducing our new mascot . . .

Then he held up Waddles—MY Waddles—wearing a Gideon wig and suit! And he called him Lil' Gideon Junior!

What had he done to him?

What had Gideon done to my Waddles?!?

I'm pretty sure Gideon had no idea what he had unleashed.
No, he didn't! Gideon was a monster—
a MONSTER!

WHACK!

I would have tried to stop Mabel, but that just wasn't possible. She was **so angry** at Gideon for taking Waddles! I don't blame her, either. So she **rushed** the stage and **kicked over** a wooden cutout of Gideon.

Grunkle Stan rushed the stage, too, and he took Gideon's podium. "**Listen up, people!**" he said. "**Gideon is a fraud!** This kid broke in and stole my property!"

"**Arrest him, officers!**" I shouted. Because that's what you shout when someone takes your pig! And not just a pig—Waddles, the **BEST PIG EVER!**

And I shouted, "Yeah!"

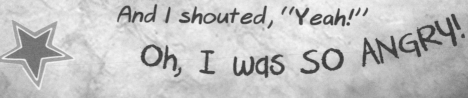

Oh, I was SO ANGRY!

The crowd didn't listen to Grunkle Stan. They didn't say it, but you could kinda tell that everyone there felt like they'd been cheated by Grunkle Stan somehow, and they didn't believe his story that Gideon had stolen the deed to the Mystery Shack.

So we were forced to leave and go back to Soos's grandma's house. Grunkle Stan didn't know what else to do. **He was going to send us back home!**

Then I had the terrible thought that "Gideonland" was really only the beginning of Gideon's plans. He had already used one of the journals to summon Bill. What would happen if he got **the third journal**? What sort of **terrifying power** would he unleash on Gravity Falls—and the world?

Luckily, we wouldn't have to find out! Gideon might have had the upper hand at the moment, but he didn't have . . . DUN-DUN-DUN!!!!! (That's dramatic music.)

A GRAPPLING HOOK!

Oh. I was going to say Journal #3.

We have that, too!

But if we were going to stop Gideon, we needed something other than a grappling hook gun—even something other than Journal #3. We were going to need an army.

And I knew **exactly** where we could get one: the forest! Because THAT'S where the GNOMES lived!

At first, I was like, "EW! GNOMES!" because, ew, gnomes. I hadn't forgotten how they'd captured me and tried to make me their queen. In no time, we found Jeff. Jeff the gnome. He was the guy who had wanted to **marry me**, and I said, "NO!" I guess after that, and because we had beaten them last time, they weren't in a big hurry to help us get the deed to the Mystery Shack back.

But **we were prepared!** Mabel suggested that the gnomes could get a **NEW** queen.

A new, **pretty** queen named Gideon!

Needless to say, Jeff agreed. Gnomes aren't too bright.

With our plan ready, we headed to the Mystery Shack. We stood outside the fence Gideon had put up, and saw him digging holes in the yard, like he was looking for something. As soon as he came over to us, I shouted, "Give us the deed to the shack, Gideon! Or else!"

And he said, "Am I supposed to say, 'or else what'?"

And then I said, "Yes, you are supposed to say that!" Then I paused . . . for dramatic effect.

(See, Dipper? That's how that's done.) Then I shouted, "NOW!"

That's when the gnome army emerged from the forest! Oh, you should have seen them. They were riding deer and rabbits and they had weapons made out of pine cones, and maybe if I didn't harbor an everlasting distrust and dislike of gnomes based on my past experience, I would have enjoyed it more.

What happened next is less impressive. The gnomes went right after Gideon, but then he pulled out a strange gold whistle. He blew into it, and it made the gnomes stop. **The sound hurt their ears!**

Gideon blew the whistle again, and the gnomes agreed to do **anything**— even turn on us—if he would just **stop!**

So WE got captured by the gnomes.

And Journal #3 fell out of my pocket.

Gideon was SO **excited.**

That was what he **really** wanted, and I brought the journal right to him!

That's pretty ironic, huh? I'm **not** a big fan of irony. Me neither!

Gideon ordered the gnomes to take us away. Without the journal, I didn't know what to do. That was where all my great plans came from! With no other options, Grunkle Stan had bought us two bus tickets. He said he couldn't take care of us without a job and that the best thing was for us to go home.

We weren't on the bus very long, though, before I saw something really weird.

You're obviously talking about the game of Bus Seat Treasure Hunt we played. Remember I found a Canadian coin and a piece of gum that was shaped like Ronald Reagan's head and—

I was talking about the giant Gideon robot that was chasing the bus.

Oh, that.

For whatever reason, Gideon had decided he still needed us! Lucky for us, it turned out that Soos was driving the bus. He told us that he'd been a bus driver for at least forty minutes, so we didn't have anything to worry about.

Soos drove us up a mountain, with the Gideon robot right on our tail. We went higher and higher until we came to a sheer cliff. The only way across was on these rickety old train tracks! Soos stopped the bus in time, so we didn't go over the edge. But Gideon showed up in his robot and tore the roof off the bus!

Mabel and I got out of the bus and scrambled across the rickety rails. On the other side was a tunnel with a sign that said DEAD END. I knew things were bad, but I didn't really need them spelled out like that.

I know, right? It was a little bit much.

Gideon followed in his Gideon robot, crossing the tracks.

Tell me! Where is Journal Number One?!?

But I didn't know what he was talking about! I told Gideon that he took the only journal I ever had. And what did he even WANT with those journals, anyway?

Apparently that wasn't the answer Gideon wanted, because he tossed me aside! Now he had Mabel. Who knew what Gideon would do? I couldn't let him hurt my sister. I just couldn't! Even if I didn't have my journal, I was still Dipper Pines, and I could make a plan!

And my plan was . . . attack Gideon!

I'M FUZZY!

CRASH!

And it was a really good plan, too! Because Gideon controlled the robot just by moving. So every time Dipper made Gideon throw a punch at himself, the Gideon robot punched itself!

I'm not sure that was my plan exactly, but it certainly worked out that way!

Gideon punched himself so hard that the robot toppled off the cliff! If it hadn't been for Mabel and her **grappling hook,** we would have been done for!

see? See? **See?**

I just gave you credit!

Anyway, Gideon also survived the fall. He tried to convince everyone that we had attacked him. But Grunkle Stan showed up and revealed how Gideon was able to pull off his "psychic" tricks. It was those Gideon pins he gave everyone!

They were hidden cameras!

Gideon had been spying on **everyone** in town and using the information he got for his own sinister purposes.

Gideon was charged with conspiracy, fraud, and breaking the hearts of **everyone** in Gravity Falls. Except for my heart. And Dipper's. And Soos's. And Grunkle Stan's.

The end!

YOU READ IT HERE FIRST, KID WHO'S HOLDING THIS BOOK:
I SAVED THE DAY! ME! STAN PINES!
OH, AND IF YOU'RE AN ADULT HOLDING THIS BOOK, GIVE IT
BACK TO THE KID. DON'T BE A JERK. ANYWAY, ONCE
ALL THAT GIDEON NONSENSE WAS OVER, DIPPER SHOWED
ME THE BOOK HE HAD, JOURNAL #3.
I TOLD HIM IT WAS ALL JUST A BUNCH OF FANTASY
NONSENSE, AND I TOOK THE BOOK.

THE KID PROTESTED, SAYING IT WAS REAL. Ha! CAN YOU
IMAGINE THAT? THINKING THAT A BOOK FULL OF STUFF LIKE

"BUTTERNUT SQUASH WITH HUMAN FACE AND EMOTIONS"
WAS A REAL THING?

WHAT AN IMAGINATION.
THEN I WENT TO
MY SECRET BASEMENT LAB.
Y'KNOW, LIKE YOU DO.

THAT'S BECAUSE THE BOOK **WAS** REAL. OF COURSE IT WAS REAL! WHY WOULDN'T BUTTERNUT SQUASH WITH HUMAN FACE AND EMOTIONS BE REAL? LOOK, YOU'VE GOT A LOT TO LEARN.

FOR THE FIRST TIME IN, WELL, FOREVER, I HAD ALL **THREE** JOURNALS: JOURNAL #1, JOURNAL #2, AND NOW JOURNAL #3! EACH JOURNAL HAD PART OF A BLUEPRINT FOR A **VERY MYSTERIOUS MACHINE**, WHICH I JUST SO HAPPENED TO HAVE BUILT IN MY SECRET LABORATORY.

LIKE YOU DO.

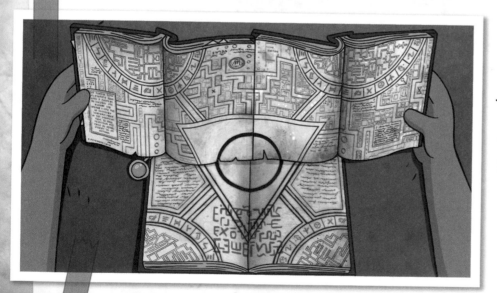

WITH ALL THREE BOOKS, I COULD MAKE ADJUSTMENTS AND USE THE MACHINE.

OKAY, NOW IF YOU TELL **ANYONE**, I'LL FRAME YOU FOR BANK FRAUD.

THE END!

SCARY-OKE

So far our summer in Gravity Falls is a blast. Dipper and me have fought and defeated several hundred forms of paranormal evil.

When we first came here, I was kind of nervous, but I was **totally** wrong to be. Grunkle Stan seemed pretty strange at first, but now that I've gotten to know him a little better, he's still pretty strange. Plus I get to hang out with Dipper a lot. We're probably better friends than we've **ever** been. That's because having a twin is like having a friend who has to like you no matter what!

I guess what I'm saying is I **love** all these weirdos. Everything's finally perfect!

Everything was so perfect,
in fact, that we decided to throw a
HUGE party to celebrate the
grand reopening of the Mystery Shack!

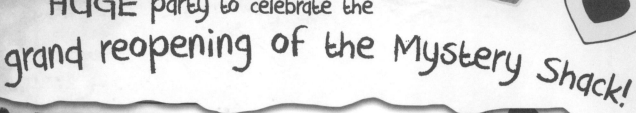

Like all great parties, it was going to have
lots of glitter and plenty of air horns.
Dipper **loves** air horns!

I don't like air horns nearly as
much as you think I do!

Why in my ears, Mabel? WHY IN MY EARS?!?

Methinks my twin brother doth
protest too much!

Grunkle Stan put me in charge of the party. He said it was because I screamed at him until he said yes, but I like to think it's because I'm an amazing party planner. I guess it's just one of those "agree to disagree" kind of situations!

LOVE PATROL ALPHA!

"MR. PARANOID"   "THE OLD ONE"   "THE HEARTBREAKER"

I dug into my bag of party tricks and decided we'd sing karaoke!

Except we were going to call it scary-oke! EVERYONE loves karaoke, almost as much as air horns! That's just a proven scientific fact! I even gave everyone a cool karaoke nickname.

"Mr. Paranoid"? Really? I mean, you're not wrong, but . . .

Dipper wasn't so sure about the karaoke.

"Wasn't so sure"? I'm pretty certain
my exact words were "Mabel, I'm not
exactly the best singer."

As I was saying, Dipper wasn't so sure about the karaoke.
But I was sure enough for both of us—sure it
would be a **great time**! Besides, I reminded Dipper
that karaoke isn't about sounding good.
It's about sounding terrible . . . **together!**

The celebration was going along just fine, if
I do say so myself. But then Soos noticed this
black car parked outside the Mystery Shack,
and Grunkle Stan kind of went nuts.

He told everyone who had come to the grand reopening to leave, and he even threatened to use the hose! He almost never does that, so you know it was serious.

The doorbell rang, and Grunkle Stan answered the door.

Two government agents were at the door! Their names were Agent Powers and Agent Trigger, and they said they were conducting an investigation. Then they just walked right into the Mystery Shack and began to look around. Grunkle Stan didn't look too happy about it.

In fact, he was acting like he had something to hide. But me? I couldn't **wait** to tell the agents all about the strange phenomena in Gravity Falls!

These agents were mysterious. I asked them if they were really investigating the mysteries of Gravity Falls, and all they said was

"That information is classified."

Hah! It was great! I always thought that agents only talked like that in spy movies. Turns out they talk like that in real life, too!

I tried to tell the agents about the journal, and they seemed interested. They even gave me their card so I could contact them later! But Grunkle Stan just played it off like I had an overactive imagination!

The agents turned around and left the Mystery Shack. Then Grunkle Stan put a hand on my shoulder. He said that he didn't want the agents looking around the Mystery Shack, and that he DEFINITELY didn't want me talking to them.

He took the card away!

Dipper was bummed about everything.
But I had the cure: **karaoke!** or scary-oke,
as I liked to call it—remember?

We had a **stage** and a **confetti cannon**, and
even Waddles was there, enjoying himself as only
a pig could do! Y'know, just by being himself!

With Grunkle Stan distracted by Mabel, who
was talking about karaoke, I decided to find
the agents' card so I could contact them.
Wendy said that Grunkle Stan sometimes hid
stuff in his room. So that was where I was
going to look first!

I **snuck** down the hallway to his bedroom. I cracked the door open slowly and then crept inside. But in a totally **non-creepy** way. I guess "crept" was a poor choice of words.

Anyway.

GOLD CHAINS & OLD MEN MAGAZINE

Cologne

I looked around the room but only found **weird** stuff, like brass knuckles and copies of "Gold Chains for Old Men" magazine.

It all seemed a little off to me. I just couldn't figure out why somebody like Grunkle Stan would have all that **stuff**. So I kept digging through it. Then I found it, hidden behind a portrait of Grunkle Stan: a box labeled "contraband"! And inside the box, I saw **the agents' card!**

I picked up the phone in Grunkle Stan's room and called them.

If you're **wondering**, I said, "This is Dipper. I have that journal I wanted to show you."

In that moment, I felt like a real spy. But again, in a **totally** non-creepy way.

But of course, what should happen next?

Grunkle Stan caught me on the phone! He wanted to know why I had called the agents, and he told me that there was nothing supernatural going on in Gravity Falls. How could he say that? He had seen so much of it himself!

Grunkle Stan was **really** mad. He told me that my "obsession" was going to get us all in trouble one day. I guess I pushed him too far. He told me to enjoy the rest of the party, because after that, I was gonna be grounded!

Grunkle Stan was right! You should have been out there at the **party** with me, Dipper! Everything was going great, and everyone was getting into the groove!

The old guy who saw the Gobblewonker was there, and he was really cutting a rug! (That's old-school slang for dancing.)

A couple of police officers showed up, too. I asked them if there was a problem. It turned out they just wanted to come in and **have fun!** So I gave them a couple of party favors and said,

"Welcome to your dreams!"

I'd never seen Grunkle Stan so **angry** before.
He'd never grounded me before. It seemed like
a pretty strange time for him to suddenly act
like a grown-up.

Even though he had told me to go out and enjoy the
party, I knew what I had to do. Grunkle Stan would
explode if he found out, but I went outside
anyway to meet with the agents when they arrived
at the Mystery Shack.

The agents didn't believe the journal was real. They even said it looked like some junk from Grunkle Stan's gift shop.

I had to prove to the agents that it was real—that all of it was real. So I read a few words from a page of the journal:

"Corpus levitas! Diablo dominus! Mondo vicium!"

Then the ground started to shake, the wind blew ominously, a giant crack in the Earth opened, glowing light burst forth, and a **terrifying** zombie crawled out.

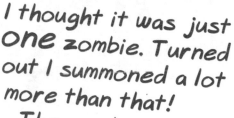

I thought it was just **one** zombie. Turned out I summoned a lot more than that! The zombies dragged the agents away. What had I done?!?

Silly Dipper. It's NEVER "just one zombie"!

Things kept getting worse. The zombies ruined Mabel's party just when she was getting to the part where she shouts "Mabel" and then the crowd shouts "Pines." She really likes that part, too.

The zombies chased me into the Mystery Shack. Soos said he'd been training for that moment his entire life, because he'd seen so many horror movies. He knew everything there was to know about how to avoid zombies. Except the part about how to avoid getting bit, because he totally got bit by a zombie.

The next thing we knew, zombie Soos was asking to eat our brains!

Suddenly, Grunkle Stan showed up with a baseball bat. He took us up to the attic, where I guess it was sort of safe, maybe, kind of?

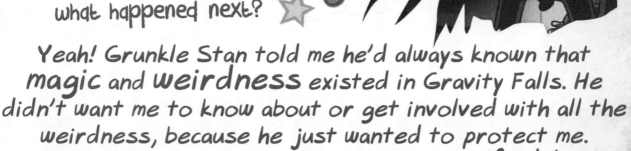

The zombies **didn't** ruin my party, Dipper! Remember what happened next?

Yeah! Grunkle Stan told me he'd always known that **magic** and **weirdness** existed in Gravity Falls. He didn't want me to know about or get involved with all the weirdness, because he just wanted to protect me.

I'd been using the journal all summer to **fight monsters,** and the only way we were going to survive was if I used it right then. So I opened the journal and turned to the entry on zombies. It turned out the only thing that could stop them was **shattering their skulls.** And the only way to do that was with a **perfect three-part harmony.**

In other words . . . **Singing!**

Lucky for us, I had brought the karaoke machine with me!

It was **glorious!** We sang until the sun came up! The three of us! Together! **The party was saved!** And also the zombies were destroyed!

But **mostly the party was saved!**

Dipper apologized for ruining everything, but I said, "Are you kidding me? I got to sing karaoke with my two favorite people in the world! No party could ever top that!"

When it was all over, Grunkle Stan decided I had done such a **great job** of handling myself with the zombies that he could trust me with the journal. So I guess it was a good party after all!

Oh, and we eventually turned Soos back to normal, but not before he tried to eat Grunkle Stan's brain.

The end!

LET'S GET a COUPLE THINGS STRAIGHT, OKAY?

BECAUSE I THINK I KINDA CAME OFF LIKE a JERK IN THAT STORY DIPPER AND MABEL WERE TELLING. IT'S NOT ENTIRELY INACCURATE, MIND YOU. IT'S JUST THAT I'M NOT SOME KIND OF CARD-STEALING MONSTER. I ONLY WANTED TO PROTECT THE KID, ALL RIGHT? HE EVEN TOLD YOU SO HIMSELF! IF ANYTHING HAPPENED TO EITHER DIPPER OR MABEL UNDER MY WATCH, I'D NEVER FORGIVE MYSELF.

ALSO, I GOTTA BE **HONEST.** I FIGURED THAT THOSE AGENT BOZOS HAD BOUGHT MY STORY ABOUT DIPPER HAVING AN "OVERACTIVE IMAGINATION." NEVER IN A MILLION YEARS DID I THINK THEY WOULD **ACTUALLY** SHOW UP! SO I GUESS IN A WAY, THE ZOMBIES SUDDENLY APPEARING WAS KIND OF A GOOD THING. IN A WAY.

Y'KNOW, FOR A GUY WHO LIKES TO SWING A **BASEBALL BAT** AT ZOMBIES.

OH, YEAH, AND ANOTHER THING! I'D DONE A REALLY GOOD JOB OF
NOT SINGING KARAOKE THE ENTIRE NIGHT. HOW GOOD?
I DIDN'T SING AT ALL! BUT THEN THE ZOMBIES SHOWED UP,
AND DIPPER DISCOVERED THE ONLY WAY TO STOP THEM WAS BY
SINGING, SO THEN I DIDN'T HAVE A CHOICE. I HAD TO SING TO MAKE
IT ALL STOP. ME. SING! CAN YOU BELIEVE IT?

I SUPPOSE I SHOULD BE PRETTY
MAD ABOUT THAT, CONSIDERING
HOW I FEEL ABOUT SINGING. BUT
I'M NOT. I GUESS I KINDA LIKE
THOSE KIDS.

NOW GO AWAY.   THE END!

SOCK OPERA

I had been waiting all summer for this moment. We found the laptop of the person who wrote Journal #3!

The thing was pretty old, but Soos said that it should work. Then we plugged in the laptop at the library. It actually turned on! In just a few seconds, its secrets would be revealed!

At first, the screen flickered and said WELCOME. But then that message disappeared, and we got an UNAUTHORIZED ACCESS FORBIDDEN warning.

Then it asked for a password.

It was eight letters long.

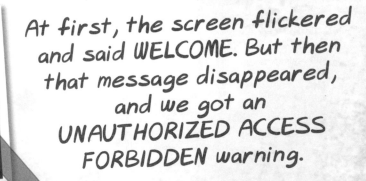

Mabel said that between my brains and her laser focus, we could solve anything. Nothing would keep us from guessing the password! So I looked through the stacks of books and found one on code breaking. I learned a lot about the subject from reading the book, but mostly I learned that there are 7.2 million eight-letter words.

We would have to try them all if we were going to break the code and get into that laptop!

I asked Mabel to read the words to me while I typed, but she wasn't there.

Oh, I was there, all right—there with Gabe,
master of puppets! Because while Dipper was
looking through the code book, I saw Gabe
putting on a puppet show for a bunch of kids.

It was magical!

So was Gabe.

I introduced myself and told him how much I
loved puppets. It's entirely possible that I
described myself as "puppet crazy" and told him
that people called me "puppet-crazy Mabel."

"So when's your next puppet show?" Gabe asked. He said
I couldn't REALLY love puppets until I put on **my own**
puppet show. Right then, I knew what I had to do . . .

*I think this is the **exact moment** when maybe
things started to go off the rails just a little.*

. . . write and compose a sock-puppet rock opera with lights, original music, and live pyrotechnics by Friday! How hard could that be, right?

I asked Dipper to help. I knew that he really wanted to unlock the laptop, and that it was really important to him. So I promised him that if he helped me fulfill my puppety ambitions just for a couple of days, I would absolutely, most definitely help him find the password.

I agreed, but only because Mabel looked at me and her eyes got real big and she whispered . . .

IT'S FOR LOVE, DIPPER.

There was no time to waste, so we got to work right away! We decided the play would be called "Glove Story: A Sock Opera." I was so excited. People's eyes were going to be wet from crying from laughing from how tragic it was! It's amazing what you can do with puppets when you set your mind to it!

So there I was, wanting **desperately** to crack the code on the laptop, but instead, I was helping my sister make puppets. I inhaled so much glitter that I think I got **glitter lung,** which Mabel claims is not a thing.

It isn't!

We worked all day and into the night on those puppets. It felt more like several days and several nights, but I think that's just how it is when you're working with puppets.

Anyway, when Mabel went to sleep, I stayed up late, trying to figure out the password. But every time I tried a **new code**, I got the same message—

ACCESS DENIED!

I wished that there was some kind of a shortcut or a clue, or that there was somebody who knew about secret codes.

Suddenly, the wind picked up, and I saw something appear. Not something, though. Some<u>one</u>. It was Bill! He said there were no hard feelings after he tried to help Gideon destroy Grunkle Stan's mind. Then he offered to give me a hint for the password . . .

. . . in exchange for what he called a "small favor."
But I told him I'd never do **a favor** for him!

Then I reminded him who defeated him last
time. (It was me, by the way.) Bill left and said
he'd be back if I changed my mind.

Actually, what he said was . . .

But I knew I wouldn't change my mind.
I mean, I had Mabel to help me

break the code!

At least, I THOUGHT I had Mabel to help me break the code. The next morning, she was STILL working on her puppet show. I told her all about the dream I had about Bill, because that's what I figured it was—just a dream.

I even mentioned the part about Bill offering to give me the secret code if I just did a favor for him. But I told Mabel that I would never do that, because I **knew** she was going to help me that day!

But I couldn't help! Not then! Gabe stopped by and told me how much he expected from my puppet show. I couldn't let him down!

We had to up our puppet game. This sock crisis had just bumped up to a code argyle!

The laptop would just have to wait.

I was so angry. I help Mabel all the time, and all I wanted was for her to help me this one time. But she couldn't even do that! Then she said, okay, she'd help me ... with tickles! That's right, she tickled me— with a puppet. I couldn't help myself, and I laughed.

But I was still really mad. So I went back to the attic and kept on trying passwords. Finally, a message came up on the computer screen. It said

TOO MANY FAILED ATTEMPTS. INITIATE DATA ERASE IN 5 MINUTES!

I only had one more try left. What was I going to do? If I didn't get it right this time, I'd NEVER unlock the secrets of that laptop and never know more about Journal #3!

I was staring helplessly at a clock ticking down the time when I felt an eerie presence.

That's when Bill appeared again. He said he'd give me the password, and all I'd have to do in return was give him a *puppet*.

He said that one little puppet was a pretty small price to pay for unlocking the answers to all the secrets of the universe.

But I still wasn't sure. Mabel had worked really hard on those puppets. Sure, I was mad at her, but I couldn't just **give** one away. But Bill reminded me that I sacrificed stuff **all the time** for Mabel, and what had she **ever** given up for me?

I only had a little time left. Thirty seconds, to be exact. So I decided to take Bill up on his offer. After all, it was only **one** puppet.

We shook hands on it, and then I asked him what puppet he wanted. He looked at all the puppets in the attic, then said, "Eenie, meenie, miney . . .

"...YOU!"
The next thing I knew, I felt like I was floating outside my body, looking right at me!

Except it wasn't me. Bill was in my body! He looked at me and said...

You're my puppet now!

Then he smashed the laptop!

Bill had double-crossed me and taken over my body. I watched helplessly as Bill tried out my body, smacking me—I mean, himself—in the face over and over. Then he laughed and said, "Pain is hilarious!" Bill told me that I had been getting too close to learning some big secrets, and that he couldn't have me getting in his way.

I thought I could stop Bill with something from the journal. Bill said he was going to **destroy** that, too! But he had to find it first. Luckily, I had hidden it in a place where he could **never** find it, not in a million years!

Of course, Mabel chose that moment to tell "me" that she had borrowed the journal to use as a prop in her puppet show. Bill-as-me said that he'd be there. I tried to warn Mabel, but I was just a ghost. She couldn't see or hear me!

What was I going to do? Bill had taken over my body. Well, maybe I could use something as a puppet, too, and talk to Mabel.

And what better puppet than my own Dipper puppet?

The puppet show was already going on when I got there. I took over the puppet and spoke to Mabel. More like I *freaked* her out at first. But then she got used to it!

I totally did! Dipper told me that he had made a deal with Bill, and that the weird triangle guy had tricked him. Even though my puppet show was going on and I wanted to impress Gabe, I had to help Dipper. I couldn't let him remain a sock puppet forever!

So I went to get the journal, which was onstage.

Bill was waiting for me. He wanted me to hand over the journal. He said that I should give him the book or my play would be ruined. Then he asked me . . .

Who would sacrifice everything they've worked for just for their sibling?

I knew someone who would. Dipper.

The REAL Dipper!

I figured that if Bill was in Dipper's body, then he'd have all of Dipper's weaknesses—which meant he was super ticklish!

Mabel did it!

Bill left my body, and **I was back!** Of course he vowed to return, but right then, I didn't care. I was just happy to be back where I belonged, and sorry that I'd ever doubted my sister. Nothing was more important to me than Mabel—not some laptop, not some secret code, **nothing.**

And I was so sorry that I had spent all that time **worrying** about the puppet show and Gabe. I should have been worrying about **my brother!** So I apologized to Dipper, and we fist-bumped.

Everything was going to be just fine!

The end!

NOW LOOK, I WASN'T AROUND FOR a LOT OF WHAT JUST HAPPENED. I WAS BUSY. DOING STUFF. DON'T ASK WHAT, NO ONE LIKES a BUSYBODY. ANYWAY, THE FIRST THING I KNEW ABOUT ANY PUPPET SHOW WAS WHEN I WALKED INTO THE LIVING ROOM AND SAW MABEL AND HER FRIENDS WITH a BUNCH OF PUPPETY STUFF.

IT . . . IT WAS WEIRD.

I'M GONNA BE HONEST WITH YOU. PUPPETS AREN'T MY THING. THEY HAVE THOSE EYES, THE ONES THAT FOLLOW YOU. YOU KNOW WHAT I'M TALKIN' ABOUT? LIKE, YOU'RE LOOKING AT THE PUPPET FROM ONE ANGLE, AND THEN YOU MOVE YOUR HEAD, AND THOSE GOOGLY EYES JUST TRACK. IT'S NOT RIGHT.

NO ONE NEEDS TO SEE THAT.

NOW, WITH THAT SAID, I STILL GOT ROPED INTO GOING TO THAT SHOW. I'M A GREAT-UNCLE, NOT A MONSTER. I FIGURED WHAT THE HECK, IF I SURVIVED ZOMBIES, I COULD MAKE IT THROUGH ONE PUPPET SHOW. THOUGH I GOTTA ADMIT I THOUGHT IT WAS GONNA BE A LOT LESS EXCITING THAN A PIG RACE, WHICH IS REALLY EXCITING.

BUT I WAS WRONG! IT WAS REALLY INTERESTING! ESPECIALLY THE PART WITH THE CAKE. AND DON'T GET ME STARTED ON THE FIREWORKS THAT FINISHED THE SHOW.

THEY DESTROYED EVERYTHING!

MABEL'S PUPPET SHOW WAS WAY BETTER THAN A PIG RACE.

THE END.

A TALE OF TWO STANS

Did you know that Grunkle Stan had a twin brother? I sure didn't! He stepped out of a portal one day—you know, like you do!

He looked just like Grunkle Stan, too!

THIS was the author of the journal! He had six fingers on one hand—and there was a hand with six fingers on the cover of the journal. It couldn't be a coincidence!

I had so many questions!

But questions would have to wait.

First Grunkle Stan introduced us. He said that his brother's name was Ford. Grunkle Ford wanted to know if anyone ELSE knew about the portal.

Grunkle Stan said it was just us, and also maybe the entire U.S. government.

We looked at a surveillance monitor, and we could see agents outside the Mystery Shack, storming the place. Luckily, the portal was in a secret room the agents could never find! It looked like our only option was to wait until the agents got bored and left.

You know who was gonna get bored? Not us! Because with all that time on our hands, you know what I was thinking?

STORY TIME!

Dipper and I really wanted to know what was happening. Grunkle Ford said he had some questions himself, and he called his brother Stanley! But I thought that Grunkle Stan's name was Stanford. It turned out that was really Grunkle Ford's name! "You took my name?" Grunkle Ford said. "What have you been DOING all these years, you knucklehead?"

Now I was super confused!

So Grunkle Stan agreed to tell us exactly what was going on, no more lies. Soos said that he hoped it all aligned with the fanfic he was writing, and that if it didn't, he was going to be really disappointed.

When they were kids growing up in
Glass Shard Beach, New Jersey, Grunkle Stan
and Grunkle Ford were best friends.

They even made plans to sail the world on
their own boat in search of adventure!
Maybe they'd find their own island and
hunt for treasure.

They called that boat the <u>Stan o' War</u>.
The brothers loved that boat,
and they were never closer.

But things change. By the time they got to high school, Grunkle Ford was a brainiac science guy! And Grunkle Stan was . . . well, he was Grunkle Stan. Some big shots from a science school were coming to check out Grunkle Ford's science project. If they liked it, they would offer him a scholarship to their college! It was a real big break for Grunkle Ford.

He'd be able to pursue all his science dreams!

Grunkle Stan **wasn't happy** about that. He wanted to sail the world with his brother. If Ford went to college, it would ruin **everything**.

In a fit of anger, Stan **hit** Ford's science project.

Maybe he didn't mean for it to happen, but the science project was ruined.

As you can imagine, the recruiters from the school weren't impressed with Ford's broken science thingy. They told him he wasn't "West Coast Tech material"!

Grunkle Ford realized that Grunkle Stan must have been the one who had ruined his project. So he went home, and the two brothers had a big fight. Grunkle Stan said that it had been a mistake, but on the flip side, they'd be able to set sail in search of treasure together.

But Grunkle Ford was so mad at his brother. He didn't want anything to do with the person who had sabotaged his dreams. That day, their dad kicked Grunkle Stan out of the house forever, or at least until he found a way to make a fortune.

Each brother went his separate way. Grunkle Stan thought the only way he could make everything better was to become a **millionaire**. At first, he tried **treasure hunting**, but he gave up when he found out that gold was some kind of "rare metal."

So he tried selling cheap products on TV, like the shammy of the future. He claimed that it was made of the same material astronauts used to clean up cranberry stains on the moon. Unfortunately for Grunkle Stan, his products were **terrible**, and his customers hated them.

And him.

SHAM TOTAL ONLY $

Meanwhile, Grunkle Ford went to Backupsmore University, which was not as good as the West Coast Institute of Technology, but still! **College!** Even though it wasn't his first choice, Grunkle Ford **excelled** at school. He graduated in record time and was given a **lot** of money to do important science research.

During his time at Backupsmore, Grunkle Ford had been thinking about his **six fingers** and how uncommon they were. He started to study the unusual in depth and found there was **one place in the world** with a higher concentration of unusual things than anywhere else.

That place was **Gravity Falls**, Oregon.

While Grunkle Ford was trying to fulfill his dreams, Grunkle Stan wasn't doing so well. Whatever dreams he'd had seemed to have fallen away, drifting to the ground like glitter from a **sad, decaying puppet.**

He was sort of living in his car, still trying to make it rich quick. He tried anything he could think of: lottery tickets, lottery tickets, and **more lottery tickets.**

And even though he wouldn't come out and say it, I know that he really missed his brother. They just needed to hug it out! Hug it out!

Hug train's comin' into the station!

Maybe they can hug later! In the meantime, Grunkle Ford used his grant money to buy the property on which the Mystery Shack stands today, setting up a base of operations in Gravity Falls. And guess what? He began to keep . . .

a journal!!!

From that moment on, his life was pretty exciting and full of incredible scientific discoveries. Everywhere he looked, there seemed to be anomalies: strange things like floating eyeballs, and weird creatures that could mimic coffee mugs, and . . . gnomes.

Gnomes! Shudder.

When he wasn't out exploring all the **weirdness** in Gravity Falls, Grunkle Ford wondered: what connected all these strange things, if anything? Was there some kind of dimension that was leaking **weirdness** into ours? He and his old college buddy Fiddleford McGucket decided to build a machine to help them test that theory.

The two friends created a portal that crossed dimensions. Grunkle Ford had hoped the portal would be a **beacon of knowledge**, a gateway to answers in his research into weirdness. But McGucket saw something in the portal that terrified him. He told Grunkle Ford to destroy the machine or it would **destroy us all!** That stinks, doesn't it?

But Grunkle Ford **refused** to give up his life's work. McGucket quit.

Without McGucket, Grunkle Ford realized that he still needed help to see his experiments through to the end, so he sent a postcard to Grunkle Stan. They hadn't spoken in **ten years!** Grunkle Stan traveled to Gravity Falls and saw his brother was afraid.

Ford showed him the portal and explained that he had punched a hole through a weak spot in our dimension.

So they were going to destroy the portal! Right? Because that's what they probably should have done! But did they do that?

No! They didn't!

Grunkle Ford said that the portal was his greatest achievement, and that he **couldn't** destroy it. So instead, he hid the journals he had made, the ones that contained all his research. But he gave the last journal to Grunkle Stan and told him to take it far away from Gravity Falls and hide it.

Grunkle Stan was angry. After all these years, his brother wanted to see him only to tell him to go away? The old arguments were brought up, and they started to **fight.**

Unfortunately, they started fighting in front of an active interdimensional portal, which is **never** a good idea.

Grunkle Ford was sucked into **another dimension!** In the scuffle, he had grabbed the journal from Stan. But he threw it back to his brother before he disappeared.

Grunkle Stan felt terrible about what had happened! He didn't know if his brother was dead, or alive, or in some distant galaxy. The only thing he knew was that the answer to bringing him back to Gravity Falls **MUST** be in the journal.

He spent weeks trying to bring back his brother, poring over the book. But he couldn't make the machine work. Eventually, Grunkle Stan assumed his brother's identity, kind of, and turned his brother's research center into the Mystery Shack. For fifteen dollars, you could enter and explore the world of the **strange** and **unusual!**

That's an incredible story!

What was even more **incredible** was that we completely forgot about the agents who were **upstairs** in the Mystery Shack, trying to find us!

Luckily, Grunkle Ford used a memory eraser he wired into the agents' headset frequency to wipe out their memories. Just as they were about to burst through a hidden door behind the vending machine upstairs, Grunkle Ford set off a **sonic shock wave.**

The agents all **grabbed** their earpieces and hunched over. When it was finished, they just stood there, totally confused, like they had no idea what they were doing there.

Grunkle Ford convinced the agents that he was actually in charge and that they had new orders. He said that the power surges that had drawn them to Gravity Falls were actually due to radiation from an unreported meteor shower. He said that he'd take the whole mess off their hands and sent them back to Washington.

And just like that, there was officially "nothing to see" at the Mystery Shack, and they left!

As if there could ever be "nothing to see" in Gravity Falls!

The end!

I GUESS THAT'S KIND OF HOW IT HAPPENED.

EXCEPT I'M PRETTY SURE I WASN'T SO AWFUL AND EVERYONE ELSE WAS WRONG. ANYWAY, AFTER THE KIDS WENT TO BED, MY BROTHER BASICALLY TOLD ME THAT I COULD STAY FOR THE SUMMER AND TAKE CARE OF THE KIDS WHILE HE WORKED IN HIS BASEMENT LAB. BUT **THEN** HE WAS GONNA KICK ME OUT.

IMAGINE THAT! MY OWN BROTHER KICKING ME OUT OF THE HOUSE I TOOK FROM HIM AFTER I ACCIDENTALLY BANISHED HIM TO ANOTHER DIMENSION AND ASSUMED HIS IDENTITY BUT THEN RETURNED HIM TO OUR DIMENSION AFTER DECADES HAD PASSED!

SOME PEOPLE ARE SO UNGRATEFUL.

SO WE FOUGHT SOME MORE AND I AGREED TO MY BROTHER'S TERMS. BUT ONLY ON **ONE CONDITION:** THAT HE STEER CLEAR OF THE KIDS AND NOT PUT THEM IN **ANY** DANGER. BECAUSE AS FAR AS I WAS CONCERNED, THE ONLY FAMILY I HAD LEFT WAS THOSE TWO KIDS!

YEAH, IT'S HIGHLY POSSIBLE THAT I MIGHT REGRET SAYING THAT LATER. BUT WHAT WAS I GOING TO DO, SIT THERE AND TELL MY BROTHER HOW I WAS REALLY FEELING AND HAVE A DEEP, HONEST EXCHANGE OF EMOTIONS?

NOPE. NUH-UH. NO WAY.

WELL, NOW IT'S BEDTIME.

THE END.

THE LAST MABELCORN

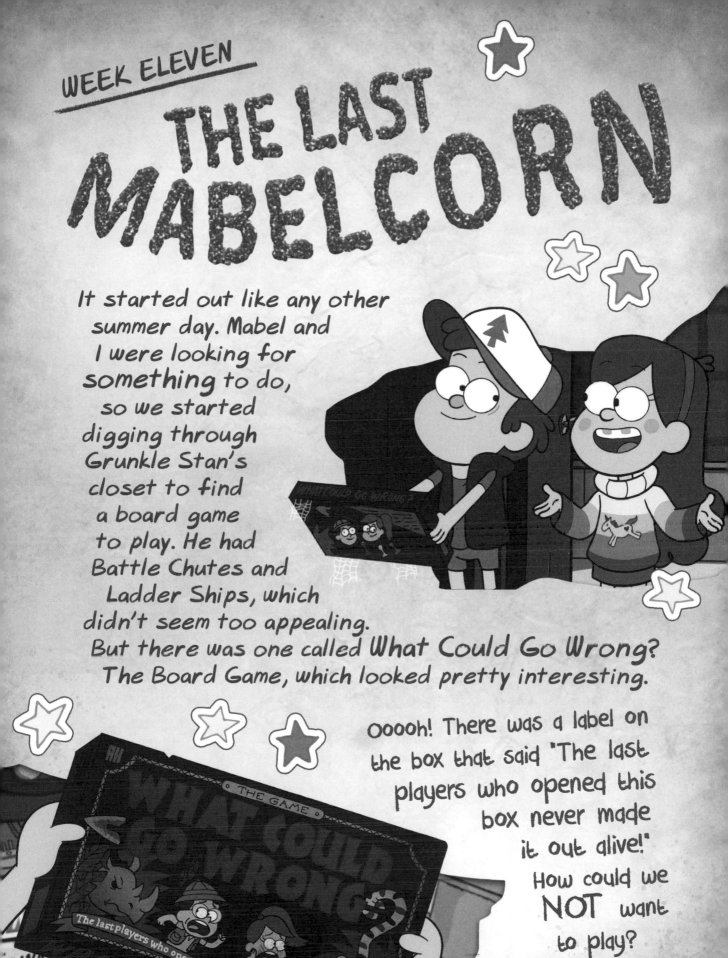

It started out like any other summer day. Mabel and I were looking for something to do, so we started digging through Grunkle Stan's closet to find a board game to play. He had Battle Chutes and Ladder Ships, which didn't seem too appealing. But there was one called **What Could Go Wrong? The Board Game**, which looked pretty interesting.

Ooooh! There was a label on the box that said "The last players who opened this box never made it out alive!" How could we **NOT** want to play?

But Grunkle Ford called a family meeting, which is not a thing we ever have. Mabel and I met him in the living room, and he had a bunch of scrolls under his arm.

The scrolls looked so mysterious! I wondered if Grunkle Ford was going to tell us that we were finally old enough to go to wizard school.

He did not tell us that we were finally old enough to go to wizard school. However, he did show us a scroll with an image of Bill Cipher on it.

I said, "Bill!"

Grunkle Ford said, "You know him?"

I said, "Know him? We defeated him TWICE!"

Mmm-hmmm! That's right! Twice!
Once with kittens, and once with tickles!

Grunkle Ford said the fact that we had encountered Bill was "gravely serious." I asked him how he knew Bill. Grunkle Ford just said that their history was complicated, but that Bill would soon return to **finish** what he had started. His powers were getting **stronger**, and if we didn't act fast, the family wouldn't be safe.

He said we needed to make the Mystery Shack "Bill-proof" so his tricks couldn't hurt us. All we had to do was place moonstones around the shack and get some mercury and . . . wait for it . . . maybe you could do a drumroll here . . .

UNICORN HAIR!!!

But Grunkle Ford said that the task would be hopeless, because unicorns live deep in an enchanted glade. Plus, only a person with nothing but goodness in their heart could obtain **unicorn hair**. Well, I was the perfect person for that job!

I was literally OBSESSED with unicorns!

My first word was "unicorn." I once made my own unicorn by taping a traffic cone to a horse's head! Not to mention the fact that I was wearing a **unicorn sweater**!

Also not to mention the fact that I was **basically** the most pure-of-heart person in the Mystery Shack!

I'M FUZZY!

I was so excited!

I convinced Grunkle Ford to let me go on the mission to get the unicorn hair.

You offered to give him your blood. You literally held out your arm and said, *"I'll give you my blood."*

Well, he didn't take it! Besides, he must have had a lot of confidence in me, because he gave me Journal #1 and a crossbow and then he sent me on my way! There's nothing **wrong** with giving a child a crossbow, is there?

I can think of at least EVERYTHING that's wrong with that.

Grenda

Candy

Our unicorn adventure had started!

I called my friends Candy and Grenda and told them to clear the afternoon. If I was going to succeed in this epic quest, I would **need** their help. I even invited Wendy to join us. We were all so **thrilled** to meet a real live unicorn! Well, except for Wendy, who stopped believing in unicorns when she was five years old.

I checked Journal #1, and it said we were near the gnome tavern and the fairy nail salon. The journal said the only way to summon the

unicorn was to bellow an ancient chant droned only by the deepest-voiced druids of old. Grenda said she was on it, cleared her throat, and started chanting.

Wendy still didn't seem to be impressed, though. She bet me ten dollars that NOTHING would happen.

After some pretty INTENSE chanting, these stones rose from the ground, along with the most beautiful gate you've ever seen. And beyond that gate, we saw . . .

A UNICORN! It was so beautiful! The airbrushed paintings on the sides of vans didn't BEGIN to do this gorgeous animal justice. We were all in awe of the unicorn. I'm positive Wendy was in awe, too, because she groaned and gave me ten dollars!

Woo-hoo, unicorn money! After a moment, the unicorn turned around and looked at us. Then she said . . .

Hark! Visitors to my realm of enchantment!

Oooh! A realm of enchantment! This day was getting even better! Her name was Celestabellabethabelle, and she was the last of her kind!

Celestabellabethabelle asked us to come in but to take off our shoes first. She had a whole thing about shoes. We told the unicorn that we needed her hair to keep my family safe. The unicorn agreed and asked the person **with a pure heart** to come forward.

I took a step forward and said, "Presenting . . . bum-ba-da-bum-bum-bum! . . . Mabel!"

Then Celestabellabethabelle's horn started to **glow**. She said that a unicorn can see deep inside a person's heart.

You have done wrong! Wrong, I say!

Well, THAT was wrong! I'm, like, the **sweetest person ever**. The unicorn told me that she wouldn't give me the hair—not until I had atoned for whatever it was I had done!

The girls all tried to cheer me up. Grenda
said I shouldn't let it get to me.

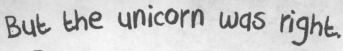

But the unicorn was right.

I used to be sweet as gumdrop sunshine,
but recently I'd been slacking in the whole
goodness department.

So right then and there, I vowed to become
a new Mabel, a better Mabel—a Mabel
who was going to get that unicorn hair!

The girls and I journeyed back into downtown Gravity Falls
and started to do good deeds. I rescued some snails from
a sidewalk! We planted trees—well, tree, singular. Still!
What a nice thing to do! And I donated blood!
So much blood! I got pretty woozy.

I had done **so many** good deeds, I figured I had erased all the bad things I had done! You know—BOOM!—karmic balance restored and **everything!** I just knew when we went to see the unicorn and she looked at my heart, she was going to say that I was absolutely a good person.

But when we went back to the unicorn's secret garden, she told me that I STILL wasn't a good person.

She wasn't going to give me the hair!

I was all like, "Booyah! Wait, **what?**"

Wendy was even more upset. She said, "How is that even **possible?**" And then she called the unicorn . . . well, she called her something you shouldn't call a unicorn!

WOW.

I didn't know what else to do. But Wendy did. . . .

Without telling me, Wendy went off with the girls and made a deal with a shady gnome to get **fairy dust**—the only thing that could put a unicorn to sleep!

Yeah, that's right—Wendy **wasn't** playing. Once they had the dust, they snuck back into the unicorn's garden and knocked Celestabellabethabelle out! They were going to take her hair **without** the unicorn's permission!

I tried to stop them, but I **accidentally** woke up the unicorn. Celestabellabethabelle was **so mad**. She thought I was the one trying to cut off her hair!

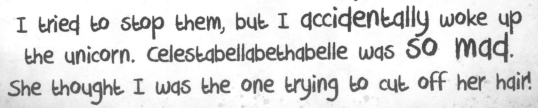

I tried to explain that it was just a misunderstanding, but Celestabellabethabelle called me a thief! A thief! Me! Mabel Pines! For shame!

Then two more unicorns entered the garden. They said that the whole "you're not pure of heart" thing was just a SCAM Celestabellabethabelle made up! The other unicorns told her that what she was doing was really messed up. Unicorns can't see into people's hearts! All their horns can do is glow, point toward the nearest rainbow, and play rave music. And to think that all that time, I thought I was a bad person and wouldn't be able to save my family.

It turned out that unicorns were jerks!

Celestabellabethabelle said, "Okay, fine, so you learned our secret. We're jerks, okay? We have more hair than we know what to do with, and we keep it to ourselves, just to tick humans off. What are YOU gonna do about it? Huh? Huh?"

Well, I was just SO mad. I'll TELL you what I did about it. I punched Celestabellabethabelle! In the face! That's right, I straight up started a unicorn fight!

Go, Mabel!

Join the dark side!

Fight! Fight! Fight!

One way or another, this was going to end.

Oh, you want to know how it ended?

It ended with me coming home with a **big ol' mess of unicorn hair!** (Also some unicorn tears and unicorn eyelashes, but that's **not** important right now.)

We even brought back a big chest full of ancient unicorn treasures! Grunkle Ford was really **impressed!** He said with all the unicorn hair we got, he'd be able to protect the Mystery Shack from Bill, no problem. He could make it so Bill's tricks wouldn't be able to affect us at all!

Hopefully!

I was so happy. Grunkle Ford told me that I'd helped protect the family. He even said I was a good person! But after that whole bit of business with the unicorns, I had come to realize that morality was relative. That's kind of a bummer lesson to learn, I guess. Oh, well. Unicorns, yay!

Thanks to Mabel, we were able to make a **protective circle** that wrapped around the Mystery Shack.

As long as we were inside the circle, Bill wouldn't be able to hurt us.

We could rest easy!

Until we couldn't. But that's another story.

The end!

YOU'RE PROBABLY WONDERING WHERE I WAS DURING ALL THAT UNICORN STUFF. WELL, FIRST OF ALL, MIND YOUR OWN BUSINESS. DID I ASK WHERE YOU WERE OR WHAT YOU WERE DOING? NO, I DIDN'T. I RESPECTED YOUR PRIVACY, WHICH IS MORE THAN I CAN SAY FOR YOU.

SECOND, MAN, I HATE THOSE UNICORNS. THEY THINK THEY'RE SO COOL, AND WITH THAT HAIR? UGH, FORGET IT. THEY'RE MORE OBNOXIOUS THAN GNOMES, AND THOSE GUYS ARE THE WORST. WELL, MAYBE ZOMBIES ARE THE WORST. THE WAY THEY LOOK AT YOU, ALL GLASSY-EYED AND UNDEAD-Y? NOT A FAN.

YEAH, SO, I WAS PROBABLY DOING SOMETHING REALLY IMPORTANT. Y'KNOW, AS BEFITS THE OWNER OF THE MYSTERY SHACK.

YEAH, THAT'S RIGHT. REALLY IMPORTANT.
YOU GONNA MAKE SOMETHING OF IT?

LOOK, MYSTERY SHACK'S CLOSED.

GO HOME.
READ a BOOK.
GO TO BED.

THE END!

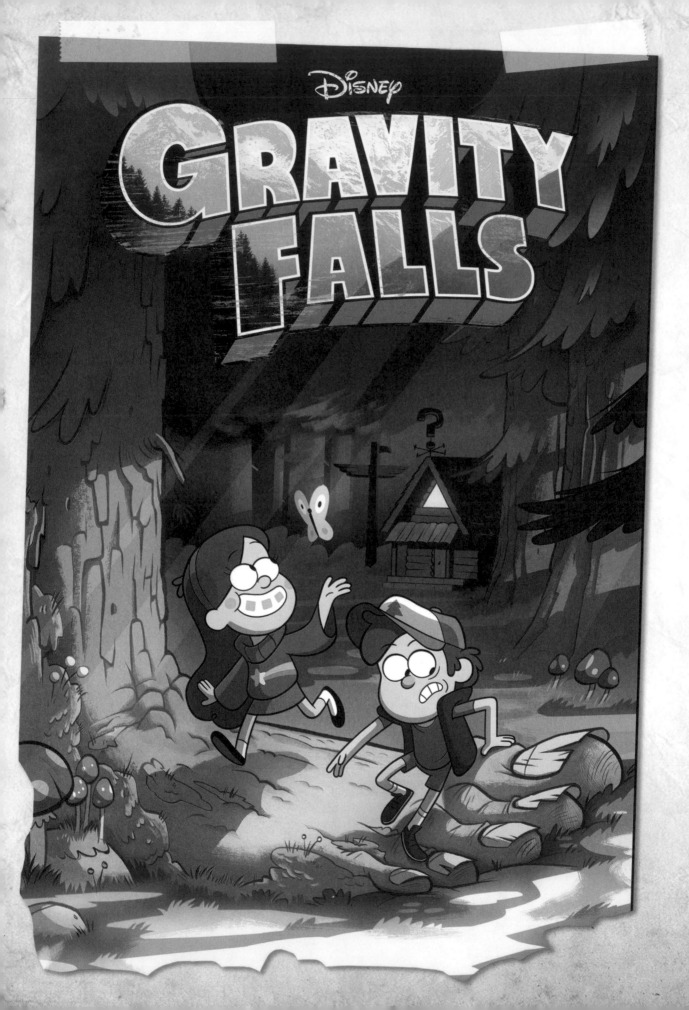